GET A

WITH JUST O...

$50 VALUE

◆ **Hotel Discounts** up to 60% at home and abroad ◆ **Travel Service -** Guaranteed lowest published airfares plus 5% cash back on tickets ◆ **$25 Travel Voucher** ◆ **Sensuous Petite Parfumerie** collection ◆ **Insider Tips Letter** with sneak previews of upcoming books

You'll get a FREE personal card, too. It's your passport to all these benefits— and to even more great gifts & benefits to come!

There's no club to join. No purchase commitment. No obligation.

SR-PP6A

Enrollment Form

☐ *Yes!* I WANT TO BE A *PRIVILEGED WOMAN.*
Enclosed is one *PAGES & PRIVILEGES*™ Proof of
Purchase from any Harlequin or Silhouette book currently for
sale in stores (Proofs of Purchase are found on the back pages
of books) and the store cash register receipt. Please enroll me
in *PAGES & PRIVILEGES*™. Send my Welcome Kit and FREE
Gifts -- and activate my FREE benefits -- immediately.

More great gifts and benefits to come.

NAME (please print)
_____

ADDRESS _____ APT. NO _____

CITY _____ STATE _____ ZIP/POSTAL CODE _____

📖 **PROOF OF PURCHASE** SAMPLE ONLY

**NO CLUB!
NO COMMITMENT!**
*Just one purchase brings
you great Free Gifts and
Benefits!*

Please allow 6-8 weeks for delivery. Quantities are limited. We reserve the right to
substitute items. Enroll before October 31, 1995 and receive one full year of benefits.

Name of store where this book was purchased_____

Date of purchase_____

Type of store:

☐ Bookstore   ☐ Supermarket   ☐ Drugstore
☐ Dept. or discount store (e.g. K-Mart or Walmart)
☐ Other (specify)_____

Which Harlequin or Silhouette series do you usually read?
_____

Complete and mail with one Proof of Purchase and store receipt to:

U.S.: *PAGES & PRIVILEGES*™, P.O. Box 1960, Danbury, CT 06813-1960

Canada: *PAGES & PRIVILEGES*™, 49-6A The Donway West, P.O. 813,
North York, ON M3C 2E8

SR-PP6B

▼ DETACH HERE AND MAIL TODAY! ▼

"We can't take this any further, Drew."

This was the part he'd been dreading. "Because of your son."

Laine nodded slowly. "If Cody thought we were…that there was a chance we might, you know, be serious…"

"Which we're not even considering." That's exactly what he'd been telling himself. So why did the words stick in his throat?

"Right…I mean, you're a wonderful person, but I don't think you're the right person for me."

"Laine…" He took her hand. "I've never been good at relationships. Not long-term. I wouldn't want Cody—or you—to end up hurt once things were over."

She nodded. This was the way it had to be, for both of them. So why did she look as if she wanted to cry, and why did he feel as though his heart were breaking?

Dear Reader,

Favorite author Kasey Michaels starts off the month with another irresistible FABULOUS FATHER in *The Dad Next Door*. Quinn Patrick was enjoying a carefree bachelor life-style until Maddie Pemberton and her son, Dillon, moved next door. And suddenly Quinn was faced with the prospect of a ready-made family!

A BUNDLE OF JOY helps two people find love in *Temporarily Hers* by Susan Meier. Katherine Whitman would do anything to win custody of her nephew, Jason, even marry playboy Alex Cane—temporarily. But soon Katherine found herself wishing their marriage was more than a temporary arrangement....

Favorite author Anne Peters gives us the second installment in her miniseries FIRST COMES MARRIAGE. Joy Cooper needed a *Stand-in Husband* to save her reputation. Who better for the job than Paul Mallik, the stranger she had rescued from the sea? Of course, love was never supposed to enter the picture!

The spirit of the West lives on in Pat Montana's *Storybook Cowboy*. Jo McPherson didn't want to trust Trey Covington, the upstart cowboy who stirred her heart. If she wasn't careful, she might find herself in love with the handsome scoundrel!

This month, we're delighted to present our PREMIERE AUTHOR, Linda Lewis, debuting with a fun-filled, fast-paced love story, *Honeymoon Suite*. And rounding out the month, look for Dani Criss's exciting romance, *Family Ties*.

Happy Reading!

Anne Canadeo, Senior Editor

Please address questions and book requests to:
Silhouette Reader Service
U.S.: 3010 Walden Ave., P.O. Box 1325, Buffalo, NY 14269
Canadian: P.O. Box 609, Fort Erie, Ont. L2A 5X3

FAMILY TIES

Dani Criss

Silhouette

ROMANCE™

Published by Silhouette Books

America's Publisher of Contemporary Romance

To Dan, my forever love

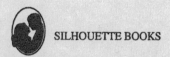 SILHOUETTE BOOKS

ISBN 0-373-19112-X

FAMILY TIES

Printed in U.S.A.

DANI CRISS

has wanted to write romance since she first read Jane Austen's *Pride and Prejudice*. In high school she dabbled in poetry and short stories, though in her mind, the words *short* and *story* are a contradiction in terms.

She squeezes her writing time between work as an office manager and taking care of her family. She lives in Kansas City with Dan, her wonderful husband of twenty-two years, her two lovely daughters, Crissie and Sara, and a varying assortment of pets.

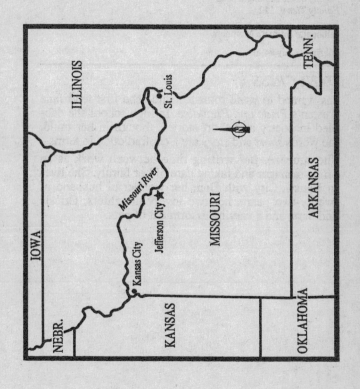

Chapter One

Drew Casteel studied the beads of perspiration dotting Arthur Masters's upper lip, concerned about his uncle's fragile state of health. As usual, Arthur hadn't mentioned how serious his physical and financial situations were.

The old man would never know how deeply that hurt. Arthur was family, Drew's only living relative. They'd been close once, but that was a very long time ago. Now, Arthur hadn't contacted Drew until ill health forced him to make this effort to guarantee the survival of his company.

"Why is it so imperative this Laine Sullivan stay with the company?" Drew asked, trying to contain his frustration.

"Laine runs this office—me included." The older man sighed heavily. "With Masters Construction in questionable financial shape—"

"Questionable is an understatement." Drew raised one black brow and slid his left hand into the pocket of his navy slacks. "Why didn't you tell me about this sooner?"

Arthur shrugged. "In the beginning, I thought the company could recoup. But the industry is down and competition is up. Even raising my bids as high as possible and putting a superintendent in the field since I can't be there, the jobs are still losing money."

Drew frowned as his uncle paused to draw in an unsteady breath. "Maybe we should cut this short. We can go over it at home tonight—"

"No," Arthur protested. "Laine and I have done all we can to get the company operating in the black again. We've tried cutbacks, closer job supervision, and a thorough audit of the books—with no luck. Things are going from bad to critical, practically right before our eyes."

Drew stiffened, angered that his uncle had downplayed the situation's seriousness for so long. Even with his heart condition he hadn't asked for Drew's assistance, and he'd discussed the problems in depth with Laine Sullivan. But not with him.

Damn it, business finance was Drew's field of expertise and Arthur knew that.

"It's obvious from the financial statements that you're operating hand-to-mouth and have been for some time," Drew said. "Keeping your creditors at bay won't be easy."

"You know the company's reputation. It's damn good. That will help you straighten things out with them. So will Laine's skills—with numbers and people."

"And I have none in either department?" Drew asked with a tight smile.

"You know what I mean. You're brilliant at pulling companies out of financial trouble. Your name's in the *Wall Street Journal* on a regular basis. And you can turn on the charm when it suits you.... But these people might balk at dealing with someone new. Especially knowing my health isn't the best. You'll need Laine as your office manager. You'll see."

What would Drew see in Sullivan? Although the audit last December showed no obvious discrepancies, it was possible the company's financial decline coincided too conveniently with the decline in Arthur's health.

For the past six months Arthur had been able to work at the office for only a few hours a day, a fact he had imparted to Drew just this morning. Sullivan had run the company almost single-handedly during that time.... Perhaps he was lining his pockets with Masters's capital.

"What if this Sullivan decides to quit?" Drew asked, keeping a watchful eye on his uncle who seemed to be weakening rapidly. He should have come back to Kansas City sooner. He would have dropped everything for his uncle, including his own business. But the old man hadn't seemed to need him.

Arthur shook his head wearily. "Laine's devoted...."

Leaving his post at the plate-glass windows, Drew walked to the mahogany desk and reached for his uncle's wrist. He realized Arthur had pushed himself as far as was safe with his serious heart condition.

Arthur pulled his hand away before Drew could get a fix on the pulse. "Just write it into the contract," he ordered, his breathing more labored than normal. "Laine stays."

Drew took a pen from his breast pocket, wrote in the words, then initialed the change and signed the contract between the two companies—all against his better judgment. Arthur needed him. His uncle would never come right out and say the words, so Drew would take what little he was given in the way of closeness and caring and pretend to be satisfied. Pretend it didn't hurt.

"Are your pills in the drawer?" he asked, his concern escalating as the older man briefly clutched his chest.

Waving Drew's hand away from the top desk drawer, Arthur grabbed the pen, added his initials beside his nephew's, then signed the document. The deal was finalized.

Drew had the sinking feeling he'd made a costly mistake. In the eight years since he'd founded Casteel Consulting, he'd pulled every client's company out of financial trouble. But if he was to be saddled with Arthur's pet protégé, he just might be facing his first defeat. And Drew did not like to lose.

But as Arthur's breathing became clearly more difficult and his color paled, Drew realized he'd had no choice but to give in to his uncle's demand.

He buzzed for the secretary, then reached into the desk drawer for the bottle of nitroglycerin tablets. He'd just located them when the office door opened and a melodious female voice made him look up.

"I'll see what Arthur needs, Mrs. Bradshaw," she said. "I want to check on him anyway."

As the woman strolled into the room Drew was treated to the sight of shapely calves, a figure that curved in all the right places, and a wealth of straight chestnut hair that just reached the collar of the hot pink jacket hugging her narrow shoulders.

She was still a couple of years from thirty, he decided as he studied her delicate features, and the aura of liveliness surrounding her. The brilliance of her smile could make a man give up everything just to please her, make him toss out schedules and miss business meetings, make him forget to breathe.

When she saw Arthur, her expression turned almost as pale as the older man's. Forgetting to close the door behind her, she rushed to his side and caught his wrist to deftly find the pulse. With a stab of hurt, Drew noted that Arthur didn't pull away from her.

"Close your eyes. Slow your breathing." As Arthur weakly complied, she loosened his tie and unfastened the top shirt button, as if she'd done it several times before. She whisked the prescription bottle out of Drew's hand, dumped two of the tiny tablets into her palm and gave them to Arthur.

He placed them under his tongue with none of the protest he would have given Drew. After a couple of minutes, when Arthur appeared to be breathing more easily, she turned her tawny eyes in Drew's direction.

"You're Arthur's nephew, aren't you?" She glared at him over his uncle's head.

Drew could only nod, his attention sidetracked by the fire in her eyes, his libido assailed by an instant and illogical wish to discover what it would be like to turn her fury into passion. He mentally shook himself, stunned that his thoughts had wandered so far, so fast. This wasn't like him at all.

"He shouldn't be upset like this." She planted her hands solidly on her narrow hips. "How long were you going to wait—"

"I'd already buzzed for Mrs. Bradshaw, but he wouldn't hear of leaving before we'd settled all the contract details," Drew informed her icily.

"In any other area, Arthur is quite capable of making his own decisions," she asserted. "But when it comes to his work, he pushes himself too far. I assumed you would know that, Mr. Casteel."

Drew stiffened. She had no right to come down on him as if he didn't feel a thing for his own uncle. "You have the name advantage over me, Ms...."

She was ready to respond when Arthur opened his eyes and raised his hand slightly. "Drew, meet Laine Sullivan."

Drew stared at her, any reply lodged in his throat. This lovely and fascinating woman glaring at him was the office manager his uncle had saddled him with.

As he watched her help the unprotesting older man to the leather sofa, Drew decided her relationship with Arthur must extend beyond the normal bounds of boss and employee. Was she an opportunist? Like Caroline?

Caro could smell money the way a shark scents blood in the water. Two years ago, Drew himself had been snared by her rare beauty, feigned innocence, and sexual charms. Watching Laine Sullivan's tender attention to his uncle ripped open the old wounds. Was she the reason the company's money seemed to be disappearing at an alarming rate? It was difficult to imagine this woman in the role of embezzler, but Caro had taught him how deceiving looks could be.

"Don't just stand there," the woman snapped at Drew, pulling him from his thoughts. "Tell Mrs. Bradshaw to get Dennis up here. Arthur needs to be home in bed."

Drew decided that for Arthur's sake he should begin cutting Laine Sullivan's ties to his uncle immediately. "I'll take care of my uncle. You tell the secretary to get Dennis on your way out."

Laine straightened to her full five-foot-three. Though Drew Casteel towered over her by an intimidating, wide-shouldered ten inches, she held her ground and locked her gaze with his cold sapphire eyes. It had been a very long time since she'd been this aware of a man's gaze. She had sensed his frank perusal as she entered the office and a thrill of anticipation had tingled down to her toes, making her senses jolt sharply to life. Then his appreciation had turned to ice.

The way she'd pounced on him for causing his uncle's current trauma must be responsible for the abrupt change, she decided. Her temper had flared instantly, as it did whenever someone she cared about was in peril. Belatedly she realized she'd gotten off on the wrong foot with Arthur's nephew.

Laine gave him a smile she hoped didn't reflect her lightning-quick attraction to him. "I realize you're concerned about your uncle, but Fred Fleming is due at two o'clock to discuss our payment schedule on his account. If neither you nor Arthur is here to meet with him, he'll file a mechanic's lien on the jobs we're doing now, and then the general contractors will hold up payment—"

"We need that money for next week's payroll," Arthur inserted weakly. "Better stay, Drew."

"Shouldn't you stay, also, Ms. Sullivan?" he asked, infuriated that, even after all these years, Arthur would take someone else's side over his. "I'll need to go over the company's current cash-flow status before I can give Fleming a commitment."

True, Laine thought. She knew that he'd just arrived and had been with Arthur for less than an hour. Not enough time to discuss the company's finances in any depth. She did need to go over the figures with him in detail, but concern for her boss, and friend, came first.

"I can see Arthur home and settled and be back here by one," she told Drew.

Before he could object, Dennis, Arthur's valet and chauffeur bustled into the room and charged toward the older man. Drew realized that their raised voices must have alerted Mrs. Bradshaw to call for the car.

"I said you shouldn't tackle this today." Dennis pinned Arthur to the sofa with iron gray eyes, his deep voice rumbling in his thick chest as he chastised the other man. "I shouldn't have let you talk me out of telling Ms. Laine how lousy you felt this morning."

Arthur winced as Laine fixed him with an admonishing look. "I had to be here today," he said on a sigh.

"Well, you won't be here any longer today. Or tomorrow," she replied. "I'll see to that personally."

Arthur shook his head. "You should stay at the office, too," he told her.

"Save your breath." She motioned to Dennis, who assisted Arthur to his feet and took his right arm. Laine took his left.

As they escorted Arthur out of the office, Laine felt the chill from Drew Casteel's thinly veiled hostility. She paused at the secretary's desk, trying to ignore her reaction to the man glowering at her from the other room. She shouldn't let him affect her, shouldn't let him get under her skin, and shouldn't regret that his attraction had cooled. But she couldn't seem to make her feelings understand that.

Mrs. Bradshaw's expression reflected her worry as she took in her employer's paleness. "I gathered things were serious so I called Dr. Manning. He wants to know whether he should meet you at the hospital or the house."

"House," Arthur inserted emphatically.

Laine had her doubts, but nodded to the secretary.

"I'll tell him," Mrs. Bradshaw said. "And the elevator's holding."

"Great." Laine let out a sigh of relief at the woman's efficiency. "Thanks."

They led Arthur toward the carpeted elevators. On the way to the lobby, he leaned heavily on Dennis. As they put Arthur into the back of the black Lincoln sedan, Laine realized how glad she was to get away from Drew Casteel's overpowering presence. She had a strong feeling there would be no working *with* him, only *for* him.

Laine groaned inwardly. She'd never dealt well with that type of person, male or female. The fact that Mr. Attitude was all male and that she couldn't seem to ignore his masculinity was going to cause her problems. She just knew it.

As the car sped through the Kansas City lunch-hour traffic, Laine thought of how different Drew was from the man seated next to her, gently holding her hand to reassure her that he would survive this episode as he'd survived the others he'd had lately. She wondered if the cold man she'd left behind was capable of the kind of concern his uncle had shown for her.

Four years ago, she'd walked into Arthur's office with only two semesters of vocational-school bookkeeping, desperate for a means of supporting herself and her five-year-old son. Arthur had given her a chance. She'd worked hard, had shown an aptitude for managing figures, and had a remarkable memory for detail. He'd rewarded her not only with raises and promotions, but with what she'd needed most at that time in her life—praise. She wondered if his nephew ever bestowed praise on anyone.

As Laine thought of the all-too-handsome man at the office, a scowl darkened her features.

"No lectures," Arthur begged, believing her glower to be for him. "Manning will scold me enough, without yours added to it."

"As if you listen to anything we say," she chided. "You know how you worry us when you do this."

He patted her hand. "I promise I'll be around awhile longer."

The big car came to a stop under an arched canopy over the semicircular drive in front of the sprawling brick house. As Laine and Dennis assisted Arthur out of the car, Dr. Manning's BMW pulled up behind the Lincoln.

"Don't give me that look, Jacob," Arthur said while the doctor surveyed his patient with an experienced eye. "I promised Laine I'm not calling it quits yet."

Arthur smiled, but it was clear he required all his strength just to make it into the house and down the hall to his bedroom. Laine left him there with Dennis and the doctor, and went to find Emma Jenkins. The middle-aged housekeeper was in the kitchen, one thin hip leaning against an oak cabinet as she made out a grocery list.

"Will he be all right?" she asked, glancing at Laine.

"I hope so."

"But he nearly did himself in, didn't he? Dennis and I both told him he wasn't up to this."

"Why didn't you call me?" Laine queried.

"He wouldn't let us. Got so irate we thought we'd better back off before we had a real problem on our hands." Emma laid her pen on the counter and turned to the refrigerator. "Tuna sandwich or a tossed salad?"

"Oh, no—"

"Oh, yes," Emma insisted. "If I let you leave with an empty stomach, Mr. Masters will give me hell about it. You eat while we wait for Dr. Manning's verdict."

"All right, make it tuna, then." Again Laine considered the contrast between the lean, balding uncle with his blue-gray eyes and caring manner, and the black-haired, cold-eyed, magnificently masculine nephew. Would Drew ever be concerned about someone in his employ missing a meal?

Once Arthur was stable, she hoped she and Drew could work out their differences, whatever they were. She'd dealt with difficult people before, but never with someone who sparked her awareness so strongly. She would have to handle her runaway physical attraction to Drew and still be able to assert herself as Arthur's office manager. They both wanted to save Arthur's company, but she had a gut feeling the nephew would want to run things his way, without her input or approval. And it might take months of working alongside the man to get Masters Construction operating in the black again.

Laine hoped their association would be limited to office hours. She wanted to be able to visit Arthur at the house as usual, without constantly encountering Drew's disapproving presence.

"Is Mr. Casteel staying at the Sheraton again?" she asked the housekeeper, praying he would be, as he had on past visits.

"His luggage came to the house this time."

Laine's spirits sank at the unwelcome news.

"Two suitcases and a very-stuffed garment bag." Emma paused to pile a mound of tuna salad onto a slice of toasted wheat bread, then continued. "I suppose he went straight from the airport to the office, as usual, but since his things were sent to the house, I assume Mr. Masters asked him to stay here."

And if he'd brought that much luggage, the visit wouldn't be brief, Laine thought. She waited until Emma placed the thickly-filled sandwich in front of her, then asked the question that had plagued her from the moment she'd felt Drew Casteel's eyes on her in Arthur's office.

"What's he like?" She could still recall the initial warmth that emanated from him before the sudden chill descended. Arthur had always spoken highly and fondly of his nephew, but the picture he'd painted didn't fit the cold man she'd met.

"Mr. Casteel?" Emma asked, glancing up. "You hadn't met him before today?"

"He's never spent more than a few minutes at the office, and he was out whenever I came by the house."

"Mr. Masters practically orders him to go out and touch base with his old friends." Emma tapped a finger to her cheek thoughtfully. "He's a real go-getter. Like Mr. Masters used to be."

"He seems so different from Arthur, in temperament at least," Laine persisted, though she couldn't say why she was anxious to learn more about the man. It was more than just a need to know her opponent, something she couldn't—or didn't want to—pinpoint.

Emma added some celery and carrot sticks to Laine's plate. "He's more reserved, a lot harder to get a handle on, but he's pleasant enough." She looked up as the kitchen door opened.

Laine glanced up also, expecting Dr. Manning. But the broad set of shoulders that filled the doorway belonged to Drew Casteel. At the sight of him, her pulse quickened despite her attempts to keep it under control.

His deep blue eyes raked over her, warm at first. A woman could get lost in that languorous heat, she thought in the split second before the warmth turned cold. She felt the chill seep in to fill her with annoyance at his manner, then her irritation changed to panic as she wondered if the doctor had called him to the house because Arthur's condition was more severe this time.

"Why are you here?" she blurted out in alarm. "Is Arthur worse?"

He arched one dark brow in surprise, then his eyes narrowed. "Since you've been here longer than I, you should be better informed about his condition."

She bristled at his tone, but forced herself to remember she would have to work with him for a long time. For that reason, and for Arthur's sake, she would try to remain civil.

"Dr. Manning's still in the bedroom." She turned her gaze back to the plate in front of her. For some unaccountable reason, she wanted to continue staring at his handsomely defined features, at the contrast of his dark blue eyes and his raven black hair. His shoulders looked strong enough to bear a thousand burdens.

It didn't seem to matter that Laine didn't want the last thought lingering in her mind. It was there to stay. The big question was, *why?* Since her divorce, she'd learned to lean on no one. She didn't need a complication like this in her life.

Anxious to take her mind off the unexpected feelings generated by the man staring down at her, she looked around for Emma, only to discover the housekeeper had made a quick disappearance in the direction of the basement pantry. Laine was alone with Drew.

Drew slid his jacket off, hooked it over the back of the chair beside her, then eased his tall frame onto the padded seat. His pale blue shirt stretched across his chest, defining the solid plane of muscle beneath the expensive fabric. He was so close, his body heat brushed against her. His cologne was spicy, tantalizing.

"Do you have a problem with tuna salad?" He glanced pointedly at her untouched plate.

That gave Laine's perspective the change it needed. "I'm not hungry after all."

Before he'd walked in with his arrogance and contentiousness, she'd considered the sandwich appealing. But between his unsettling nearness, his undeniable masculinity, and his unexplained coldness, she couldn't summon any enthusiasm for the food. She pushed the plate toward the center of the table.

Drew snatched half of the sandwich, then shoved the plate back toward her. "Eat that much at least," he commanded before taking a bite.

She stared defiantly at him, taking more time than he liked to back down under his steady gaze. Finally she reached for the sandwich and took a small bite. Drew was annoyed at the relief he felt at seeing her eat. She could use an extra pound or two, but why should he care whether she went hungry? He should hold on to his anger instead.

"I thought it was decided you would stay at the office," she said, interrupting his thoughts.

"By you and Arthur. I make my own decisions."

"Regardless of the advice of others."

"Seems the same could be said of you. Arthur suggested you stay, too." He polished off his sandwich and reached for one of the celery sticks, pointing it at her as he spoke. "You appear to have a real problem with authority, Ms. Sullivan. I suggest you get over that problem. Soon."

Laine sat in stunned silence for one long heartbeat, then gave a humorless laugh as his resentment of her began to make sense. "The last of the true male chauvinists."

"You can thin our numbers down, but you can't wipe us out completely."

She met his forceful gaze steadily. "Given the number of women in today's work force, I'd think your antiquated attitude would create a lot of unwanted friction."

"I have no problem dealing with a woman who knows her place."

"Knows her place," Laine repeated through clenched teeth. From the cradle, those words had been drilled into her head. Inwardly she'd always questioned the philosophy of male supremacy. It had eventually destroyed her marriage and alienated her from her very traditional parents. The damage to her self-confidence had been extensive, but she'd put the pieces of her life back together. She'd found her strengths and built on them until she'd learned she could hold her own with anyone. Including Drew Casteel.

"I find it surprising that a man in your position has been able to succeed in the modern business world while remaining mentally stuck in the Dark Ages, Mr. Casteel." Her eyes blazed across the table at him.

Drew didn't believe any of what he said. He was just determined to bait her. As long as they were fighting, he was in no danger of being taken in by her soft, understated beauty. He'd been taken in by a woman's good looks once before, and had learned his lesson well.

"Your social life must be severely limited, too." Laine crunched into a carrot stick, gritting her teeth as his left brow arched with disdain.

"My social life?" he asked in a disinterested tone. "How do you mean?"

"It must be quite difficult finding a woman whose IQ is low enough to suit your tastes, or one who enjoys being bashed over the head and carried to your cave every night."

Drew bit through the celery stalk with enough force to pulverize granite. He liked the excitement and energy of a good clash and didn't generally let verbal barbs get under his skin. But with Laine Sullivan the situation was altogether different.

He would break her ties with Arthur, but without forcing her resignation as he'd originally planned. Instead he would keep her under his thumb, and make her work atmosphere as difficult as possible. While he enjoyed watching her squirm, he would find out what was happening to Masters Construction's finances and whether she had a hand in the company's problems. If she did, he would have a ringside seat when the police came to cart her sexy tush to jail.

"You never answered my question as to why you're here." She finished the carrot stick and picked up her sandwich.

Drew eyed her steadily. "Dennis will need to stay here with Arthur. That leaves you without a ride back to the office. I didn't want you to have any excuse to extend your lunch hour, waiting for a taxi.''

As Laine opened her mouth to utter an angry protest, Dr. Manning walked in. One look at his lined face told her the news wasn't good.

Chapter Two

Laine gripped the edge of the table. "How bad is it?"

Dr. Manning sank into the chair across from Drew. "He'll make it. This time."

"This time," she echoed, noting Drew's worried expression. "What about the next?"

"Good question," Emma said, striding back into the room. "Fix you anything, Doc?" When he shook his head, she glanced at Drew. "Mr. Casteel?"

"Maybe later." He reached to push the fourth chair away from the table. "Sit down. I know you'll want to hear what the good doctor has to say."

Dr. Manning waited until Emma was seated. "I've given him a shot, so he'll sleep the rest of the day. Dennis is monitoring him, but I'm calling in a nurse. There need to be more life-style changes, too, starting with a wheelchair."

Laine sucked in a deep breath. "He's resisted that for

a long time. How are you going to get him to give in now?''

''He's finally accepted that he's pushing himself too hard for a man in his condition.''

Laine knew there was no cure for Arthur's condition. For him, the combination of moderate exercise, meditation, strict diet, and giving up cigarettes was all that could be done to improve the blockage in two coronary arteries. The damage to his heart muscle from previous attacks made him a poor risk for bypass surgery. She'd suffered with him each time she'd heard Dr. Manning lecture him on it. Perhaps now, he was ready to listen.

''What about a transplant?'' Drew asked anxiously. ''Isn't there any possibility?'' He knew he was probably grasping at straws, but there had to be something that could be done.

The doctor shook his head. ''Not with his age and the condition of his arteries. He simply has to cut back on his activity, watch his diet better and learn to relax. I think he's finally accepted that.''

''He's paid little attention to our lectures before now. This episode must have been bad,'' Laine said.

''Bad enough to shake him up. Someone should be with him almost constantly.''

''Between Laine, Dennis and me, we've been doing that,'' Emma told him.

''Good.'' Dr. Manning looked at Drew. ''Will you be staying at the house with him during the evenings?''

Drew nodded. At last it was clear why Arthur had finally asked his help in getting the construction company back on its feet, and why he'd agreed to let Drew stay at the house. He'd realized he was getting worse.

But why hadn't he called months ago? They could have had more time together.

"Shall I arrange for the nurse?" Drew asked the doctor.

"With Laine's agreement, I've had one agency lined up for him," Dr. Manning said.

Drew bristled at her intrusion. It seemed he would never be invited into his uncle's inner circle. But Laine Sullivan, an employee Arthur had known for a few short years, was right where Drew had wanted to be practically all his life.

Why did this type of intimate friendship come so easily for some and so arduously for him? What was the secret, what were the magic words? How had she penetrated Arthur's tough shell? And, more important, what were her motives?

"The nurse will be here this afternoon." Dr. Manning glanced at Emma. "I noticed the bottle of tranquilizers I prescribed is nearly empty. I'll write out a refill."

"He won't take them," she said. "Even though Laine pushes him."

Laine blinked in surprise. "He's always taken the pills for me."

"Because you tell him you'll worry and he doesn't want that," Emma insisted. "But the other day I found a handful of them behind the nightstand."

"That old buzzard!" Laine growled softly. "He won't get away with that trick again."

Drew scowled. The woman was a fixture around Arthur's house as well as in his office. She'd become the voice of authority to Arthur, who'd never been satisfied in a subordinate role. She was liked and respected by them all. But they hadn't had Drew's experience with

Caro. Caro had taught him so much about taking someone for all you could and he would never forget that lesson.

What if Laine Sullivan's concern for Arthur was only an act? Could Drew protect him? The old man would be crushed to learn someone he trusted had been stealing from him.

"What about Arthur going into the office?" Laine asked, trying to shake off Drew's icy gaze. "He's not going to stay home for long."

"Possibly Monday, but only for an hour and only if he rests over the weekend. I don't think he'll give us any static over it this time." Dr. Manning stood, patted Laine's shoulder, then turned to Drew and extended his hand. "You've got my number if you need me."

Drew nodded. "Any instructions for when he wakes up?" he asked.

"Just keep him down and quiet. I'll stop by on my way home from the office tonight, and again in the morning."

As Emma walked Dr. Manning to the door, Drew checked his watch. "We should get back to the office." He got to his feet, and waited for Laine to do the same.

She frowned up at him, tiny lines creasing the smooth skin of her brow. "Don't you want to look in on Arthur?"

"He's asleep. He wouldn't know I was there." Probably wouldn't care, Drew thought. How long had he wished he and Arthur could be closer, never to have that hope realized? Yet this woman could breeze in and succeed where he had failed. He wanted to beg her to tell him how she did it. He wanted to lash out at her and everyone in frustration. He wanted to guard Arthur from any harm, any hurt she might inflict. How far could he trust her seemingly genuine caring for his uncle?

"You can't be sure he wouldn't know." Laine stood and slowly pushed her chair against the table. "If it were my uncle lying in that room, nothing could keep me from seeing him before I left the house."

Drew's jaw clenched at her gently scolding tone even as he noted the alluring scent of her perfume. How could he be so aware of her? Why did he find it so difficult to hold on to his fury? "Are you saying I don't care about my uncle?" How dare she—

"I'm just pointing out that little gestures often mean a lot, and—" she fixed him with a steady gaze "—I think that even though he's not awake, on a deeper level, he can sense your caring. I'll wait outside."

She walked out, leaving Drew standing there as if planted in that spot on the kitchen floor. He ought to be headed outside to give her a piece of his mind, not following the unusual compelling need to see his uncle.

In the bedroom, Dennis sat in the wing chair beside the double bed, his eyes alternately on the monitor and the patient. Arthur slept, as Drew had expected. What he hadn't expected was the frustration and fear he felt at the thought that his uncle might cash in before he had a chance to let him know how much he cared. Would his feelings even matter to the old man?

So much had changed between them when Drew's mother had died. Drew had been eight years old. He'd needed the family connection, but his father had coped with the tragedy by throwing himself into his work; and Arthur, who had been very close to his only sister and her son, had withdrawn.

Drew understood why. Each time he glanced in the mirror, he was reminded of how much he resembled his mother. They'd all missed her unbearably, but neither his father nor Arthur had understood how very much Drew had needed them. They'd withdrawn into themselves, away from him, and none of them had been able to repair the rift. But the bonds couldn't have been very strong in the first place if they were so quickly and finally severed.

He watched his uncle sleep. Arthur's angular face appeared thinner in his relaxed state, his breathing easy and even, but his complexion was grayer than it should be. Drew swallowed hard.

"He's resting comfortably," Dennis said quietly.

Drew nodded, not knowing what he should say, not even knowing why he was here. Did he hope that his uncle would wake and the past years' emotional distance would be forgotten? That they could go back to the closeness they had shared so very long ago?

"Give the old man a couple of days in bed," Dennis told him, "and he'll be up to his old tricks."

Drew smiled. That was Arthur, all right—invincible. How many men would still be running their own company at seventy-two? How many could survive two heart attacks and hardening of the arteries and still keep plugging on?

"The man is amazing," he said. "I'll be back around six. Page me if there's any change."

Dennis nodded. "Sure thing, Mr. Drew."

With that, Drew left the bedroom. He opened the front door and found Laine leaning against the fender of his rented Mercedes coupe. He let her in, then got behind the wheel. As he pulled onto the Mission Hills street lined with upper-income, pricey homes, Drew felt some of the tightness between his shoulder blades ease. Arthur would be all right—for the time being.

"How was your uncle?" Laine asked, buckling her seat belt.

His tension returned instantly. If only he knew the root of her concern for Arthur, he would feel a lot better. "Asleep."

Laine sighed. She wanted to know how Arthur had looked. It had taken every ounce of her willpower not to go to his room, but the feeling that doing so would create more hostility between her and the King of Chill had made her wait outside. She didn't understand Drew's testiness, but the air in the navy blue coupe was charged with it.

"How was his color?" she pressed, needing to know. "His breathing?"

"Gray. Easy."

She mulled that over for a moment, her hands clenched in her lap, then turned her gaze to the side window. Drew sensed she wanted more details, but hesitated to ask.

"He'll make it," he said, feeling a need to reassure her further, a need as compelling as the one that had sent him to check on his uncle—a need he should resent. But his emotions wouldn't cooperate when she turned back to him, a brief, small smile flashing across her lovely face.

"How can he be so resilient?" she asked.

"Sheer determination."

Another tiny smile lit her face for a second. "That's Arthur, for sure. I've never known anyone like him."

Hearing the affection in her voice, Drew experienced the irrational longing to have it directed toward himself. Returning to Kansas City to find his uncle seriously ill and the construction company in financial straits had left him feeling more estranged than ever from Arthur...from everyone. That must be why Laine was getting past his defenses.

Time for a reality check. What was she hoping to gain? Did she figure Arthur would leave her a wealthy woman? That was quite possible, given Arthur's affection for her and his innate generosity. But it galled Drew to think she might be using his uncle.

"After the meeting with Fleming," he said stonily, "I want to go through the personnel files. Make copies. I'll read them at the house in the evenings."

"We don't have personnel files, per se. We—"

"Surely you have records of your employees."

She stiffened at his terse interruption. "Yes, but—"

"Then there shouldn't be any problem."

"The problem is," Laine began tightly, fed up with his overbearing manner, "construction companies generally operate more casually than other corporations you may have dealt with. If we need another man on a job, we hire the first person to phone or show up on the site. Our personnel records consist of name, address, social security number, and withholding information."

"That's the first change I'm making. I want full employment and background files on every employee." Especially on her. Maybe a thorough check would turn up something that would keep his feelings for her in line, keep him from falling for her charms.

Laine bit her lower lip to halt her angry retort to his sarcastic tone. "May I ask why you need this information?"

"No."

She bit her lip twice this time, determined she wouldn't give him the satisfaction of snapping at him. "Then may I ask when you want all this?"

"By Friday afternoon."

"Fri—! But this is Thursday."

"I'm aware what day it is."

His coolness fueled her mounting fury. "But we don't even have the forms—"

"Order them from your office supplier."

"It'll take a couple of days to get them delivered."

"Then make up your own format and type the information on plain paper."

"How considerate of you," she muttered through clenched teeth as he braked for a red light on Ward Parkway. She took several deep breaths, but it didn't dent her anger. When he merged with the Country Club Plaza's heavy business traffic, she decided she was as calm as she was going to get. "What about field personnel? Do I call them off the job and into the office for this—" This ridiculous impulse of yours, she barely refrained from saying.

"I plan to visit the jobsites this afternoon, as soon as the meeting with Fleming is over. You can accompany me and get the facts on the men there."

Great, Laine thought. An afternoon in the car with him. The very thing she didn't need. If she spent much more time with him, she would undoubtedly tell him off.

"You're being unreasonable, wanting this by tomorrow," she snapped as he maneuvered the Mercedes into the parking garage.

"A moment ago you said I was considerate."

"I was being sarcastic. Why must this be done in such a rush?"

He eased the coupe into the stall reserved for Arthur, shut off the engine, then turned to her, his left brow arched arrogantly. "Because that's what I want, and while Arthur's laid up, I'm in charge."

With that, he got out of the car. Laine sat unmoving, her defiant gaze staring straight ahead. She saw Drew take a few steps toward the building, then pause and turn back when he noticed she wasn't following. He came around to her side of the car and pulled the door open.

"Is there a problem, Ms. Sullivan?" he asked tightly.

"No problem, Mr. Casteel. I just assumed that being such a chauvinist, you would prefer to open my door yourself."

The muscle in his jaw knotted as she got out. Laine sashayed across the concrete floor, glorying in the sound of his slamming the car door.

Drew followed several paces behind her, forcing himself to maintain an even stride while he worked to control his irritation. And attraction. Her fanny swayed in a subtly sexy way, he thought, then promptly tore his eyes away from the mesmerizing sight.

She stopped at the building's doors, smiling smugly as she waited for him to catch up. Drew found himself wanting to grab her by her slender shoulders, press her against the glass panes, and wipe that Cheshire-cat grin off her face with a forceful kiss. A kiss that would bring out her fury and channel it into passion.

The mental image of her tawny eyes blazing with desire brought his thoughts to an abrupt halt. He yanked the door open, then followed her to the elevators, tamping down his hormones by concentrating on his annoyance.

Laine punched the button for the elevator rather than wait for Drew to do it. Judging from his glower, she'd pushed the man to the limit of his barely-existent sup-

ply of patience. There was a time to make a stand and
a time to play it safe. She still had to work with him.

A depressing thought, but the knowledge that she'd
scored a direct hit over the car door cheered her up
considerably. The feeling of triumph stayed with her as
they rode the elevator to the fourth floor, then walked
down the hallway to Masters Construction's suite of
offices.

What was the man's problem with her? Laine fumed
as she waited for Drew to finish his conversation with
Sam Kingston, the burly carpenter foreman. This was
the third jobsite Drew had taken her to, and at every one
she'd felt the heat of his glower as she'd gotten the necessary information from each of the workers.

The problem, whatever it was, had to be personal, she
decided as his narrowed gaze swept over her. He seemed
to get along with Arthur's housekeeper. He hadn't been
rude to Dr. Manning. He'd been quite cordial and professional with Fred Fleming. As he had been with everyone, except her.

She glanced at her wristwatch, noting it was nearly
four o'clock. They'd spent the entire afternoon together and she hadn't seen one smile, nor had one warm
word from him. Was he still angry over her panic at
Arthur's crisis?

Whatever the cause, his coldness was for the best. She
wouldn't have stood a chance against him if he'd put on
the charm. And resist him, she must. She'd been under
the thumbs of two controlling males before—her father and her ex-husband. She wouldn't put herself in
that position again.

"Laine, bet you didn't know Drew labored for me
summers when he was in high school and college," Sam

commented with a broad smile. "Of course, you wouldn't hardly recognize him now with his hair cut and him wearing a suit instead of dirty overalls."

"That was a very long time ago," Drew inserted before she could respond.

So the man hadn't been born in a three-piece suit. He'd once done manual labor for a living. His black hair was now styled to enhance his professional image, but her wayward mind conjured up an image of him with it a little longer, a little shaggy around the ears and hanging over his collar. He would look inviting, touchable, sexy, she thought, with shocking delight at the mental picture.

"We need to get back to the office," she said quickly, turning toward the car.

Drew followed silently. Glowering probably, she guessed. But she didn't turn around to find out. The sooner she was back in her nice, safe office, away from Drew and his masculinity, the better.

At the edge of the concrete slab, he took her arm to help her across the muddy path. His touch jolted her senses and left her reeling. Her steps faltered, her feet refusing to obey her mind's command to walk. She looked up to find him staring down at her. There was a flicker of emotion in his sapphire eyes, but it was gone before she could put a name to it.

Her surprise and confusion must be evident on her face. She only hoped he couldn't tell that her breath was trapped in her lungs, her pulse was racing, and her temperature had shot up several degrees. Could he feel her body heat under his hand? She knew she should pull her arm out of his grasp, but the strange and compelling urge to remain where she was won out.

Drew felt the electric charge that passed between them. His entire body responded to the contact. Stunned, he looked into Laine's eyes and saw that her expression mirrored his feelings. What was happening to him? He tugged her arm until she began to move, then, once across the muddy path, he released her to dash ahead and unlock the car.

When Laine was settled in the car, she inhaled deeply to steady her rattled nerves, but once Drew got in beside her, the interior seemed smaller than before. His thigh seemed closer to hers, so close she could feel the warmth of him. How could his mere touch send her good sense running for cover, leaving behind a startlingly strong physical attraction?

She stole a surreptitious glance at his profile. His eyes were focused intently on the road, as if he was oblivious to what their brief physical contact had done to her equilibrium. Hadn't he felt anything? Laine huddled in her seat, puzzling through the questions, but nothing about the incident made sense.

The silence stretched on as Drew nosed the Mercedes up Southwest Trafficway toward the stretch of road that would take them back to the office. In the car's close quarters, Laine's delicate flowery fragrance was impossible to ignore. Drew breathed deeply in an effort to achieve a degree of calm, only to be thwarted by the intoxicating scent. Since Caro, he'd been able to get any woman out of his thoughts with very little effort. Why, then, was Laine's nearness so damned unsettling?

He pulled into the parking garage, annoyed that she pretended nothing out of the ordinary happened when he touched her. Maybe that was for the best. Discussing what had transpired on the jobsite's muddy path would mean dealing with those feelings—something he wasn't ready to do. He didn't generally discuss his feelings at all. But something about Laine made him long to do a lot more than talk. What the hell was this woman doing to him?

Laine got out as soon as he'd shut off the engine, glad to escape the confining car. Drew's nearness was too unsettling, his silence too upsetting, her feelings too frightening. The only sounds in the coupe had been the soft music from the CD player and the hammering of her heart.

She let herself into the building, absently saying good-night to the staff heading home for the day. She raced for the sanctuary of her small office. Crissie, her nervous young assistant, spun away from one of the file cabinets in the corner, leaving a middle drawer open.

"I . . . I . . . you startled me," she stammered.

"Sorry," Laine said brusquely. She had too much on her mind to deal with Crissie's usual jumpiness.

"I was waiting for you to get back. Mrs. Bradshaw had to leave and asked me to stay," Crissie gushed, hesitantly glancing at the doorway. "She didn't know if you had a key, Mr. Casteel."

"I do. Did she leave any messages from my uncle?"

"N-no . . ."

"I'll take care of the door," Laine assured her assistant. "You can go on home."

"Thanks." Crissie's voice still trembled as she gathered her purse and umbrella. "See you tomorrow."

Laine nodded as Crissie left. Once the girl was gone, Drew phoned Emma Jenkins to ask about his uncle. Laine felt his eyes on her as she put her legal pad in a drawer, then thumbed through the day's mail on her desk. Her thoughts, though, were on him, on his stony silence once he'd hung up the phone.

"Is Arthur all right?" she asked to break the quiet.

"He's still sleeping."

She nodded and finished looking over the mail. Still he stood there, one hip perched on the edge of her desk. Why didn't he leave? Since he so obviously found her presence hard to tolerate, it didn't stand to reason that he would hang around. Nor did it seem logical that he could so easily affect her senses when she felt nothing but anger and enmity for him. Or was that all she felt?

"What is it?" he asked softly, almost tauntingly, his dark brow arched in superiority.

"What do you mean?"

"I get the feeling you have something you want to say."

Laine walked toward the file cabinet to close the drawer Crissie had left open, intending to ignore him as he had her. At the last minute, her temper got in the way. Forgetting the file cabinet, she turned to face him and force a showdown—or at least clarify one point.

"May I ask why you've taken such a dislike to me?"

The question caught Drew off guard for an instant. He couldn't tell her the truth. Not until he knew for sure what Arthur meant to her. "My reasons are my own."

"Fine," she snapped. "Then I won't ask."

"You already have."

"So I'll unask."

He shook his head at the ridiculousness of that statement. "You can't do that."

"You going to stop me?"

"This is childish," he muttered.

"Exactly." She nodded triumphantly.

He gave an exasperated groan. The woman had a sharp tongue and a quick wit. A dangerous combination—and a challenging one. It would take a strong-willed and equally quick-thinking man to tame her sass. The thought of tackling the task himself was quite intriguing.

In one swift movement, he pushed away from the desk and pinned her to the file cabinet, caging her there with his arms. Her eyes widened and her lips parted. Taking full advantage of her surprise, Drew lowered his head and captured her in a kiss.

Once Laine's shock wore off, her hesitation vanished, leaving her mouth soft, pliant, yielding under Drew's demand. He drank from it greedily, devouring the incredible sweetness he hadn't expected to find. With an urgency he couldn't fathom, he deepened the kiss, exploring the treasure he'd unearthed.

Her skin was soft. She smelled of wildflowers in April and tasted of sweet passion. As his tongue boldly entered her mouth, her breath caught, then rushed out on a moan. Drew needed no further encouragement. His heart pounded as he took what she gave so generously. His lungs clamored for air, but he refused to give up the exquisite pleasure of kissing her.

Laine raised her hands to the lapels of his jacket. She wanted to shove him away and pull him closer. She wanted to stop him and to beg him to let the kiss go on forever. She wanted to run from him and to cling to him with all her strength.

Good sense fought a halfhearted battle with need, and lost. With every breath, she inhaled the spicy scent of his cologne and longed to be closer to him. With every brush of his tongue, she felt the heat within her grow. With every moment he prolonged the ecstasy of the kiss, she became more his willing captive.

The last thought ricocheted through her mind, scattering her traitorous longings. How could she have allowed this to happen? Allowed him to break through her defenses? How could she respond to someone she disliked—and who disliked her—so thoroughly? Someone so controlling?

Laine pulled away. In the depths of his eyes, she caught the victorious gleam lurking behind the lust. He'd already proved to himself he could dominate her on the work front, and now he felt he could rule her personally, as well.

She fingered his tie, gently pulling him closer, maneuvering him into position. Then with one deft movement, she had his tie in the file cabinet and the drawer closed. She twisted the knob, locking all four drawers. She tugged at the silky fabric, pleased when it remained firmly stuck. "That should hold you until you cool off."

"Laine," he growled as she snatched her purse off the desk. "Laine..."

She patted him on the rear as she passed him. "See you, Casanova."

Chapter Three

Horrified, Drew heard Laine walk out to the foyer, shut the door behind her, and then lock it. He tried to jerk his tie out. Tried yanking the drawer handle with all his strength. To no avail. The cabinet keys were nowhere in sight on Laine's desk. To top everything off, she'd gotten enough of the tie into the drawer that he couldn't ease the knot down and slip the tie over his head.

Damn the woman and her breath-stealing kiss. She had no right to pull out emotions he'd buried long ago, then leave him like this. He hadn't even seen it coming.

He jerked at his tie again, but only tightened the noose around his neck. He dented the cabinet with his fist, angry with Laine, yet angrier with himself for letting her get past his control. She'd made him come alive, made him feel, made him crave more of the sweet passion he'd sparked in her.

But what if there was no truth in the temptress? His mind refused to contemplate the thought. He gave the tie another jerk. The fabric ripped, but remained firmly lodged in the drawer.

He had to get out. Being found in this position would turn him into the company laughingstock and make it damned difficult for him to help his uncle. Arthur was counting on him. This was the first time he'd asked for Drew's help and Drew couldn't let him down.

He stretched across the desk, hoping there would be a set of keys in the top drawer, but he couldn't reach that far. A pair of scissors perched in the pencil cup, but those, too, were out of range.

Leaning his shoulder against the cabinet, Drew tried to snag the cup with his foot. He was an inch short. Swearing, he pushed as far away from the cabinet as his bonds would allow. At last he came close to the object of his rescue, only to knock the cup over.

Pencils and pens clattered to the carpet. Swearing again, he surveyed the desk. The scissors lay with their points still inside the cup, which wobbled on its side as if debating whether or not to tumble to the floor as well.

In desperation he kicked off one shoe, extended his leg as far as he could, then worked his big toe through one of the blue plastic grips and dragged the scissors closer and closer to the edge of the desk, inch by sweating inch.

Finally freedom was at the tips of his fingers. He snagged the scissors, clutching them tightly in his hand as he cut the tie at the knot. The section inside the drawer would have to remain there. All that mattered was escape. He undid the part of the tie around his neck, pitched it into the wastebasket, then grabbed his shoe, slipping into it as he hopped to the door.

He unlocked it, stepped into the hall and out of the building. Breathing the fresh rain-scented air like a convict just released from prison, he got inside his car and pulled onto the now wet street.

As he rounded the corner, he spotted a slender figure in a hot pink skirt and jacket. Laine. Drenched, she stood in front of a rust-eaten orange Volvo, staring down at the engine, her expression a mixture of fury and bewilderment.

His heartbeat quickened as the humiliation of moments ago raced through him. The desire to run her over warred with curiosity as he stared in disbelief at the ancient vehicle. He slowed to a crawl to observe her without being seen.

This couldn't be her car. Surely with the salary Arthur paid her, she should be driving something in better shape. But no one else came to claim the rust-covered hunk of junk, and she was getting wetter. At last she slammed the hood shut, walked around to kick the front tire, then glanced up and down the street as if deciding her next course of action.

Fate had presented him an opportunity to continue his original objective—keeping an eye on her.

He would be on guard now that he knew what she could do to him. His hormones still ran wild when he recalled his too-brief taste of her lips. Vowing he wouldn't exhibit that lack of control over his emotions again, he pulled alongside her car.

He leaned across the front seat to push his passenger door open. "Get in."

Laine blinked, not fully trusting her eyesight, but when she couldn't banish the image of Drew and his Mercedes, she leaned forward to see him more clearly. "So you got loose. Too bad. I was looking forward to hearing you explain what happened when everyone came in tomorrow morning.''

''Sorry to disappoint you,'' he growled. ''Do you want a ride or not?''

She studied him warily. What did he want from her? He'd kissed her senseless, but only in the name of male arrogance and domination. Then, as if neither his hostility, nor the kiss, nor her retribution had occurred, he showed up to offer her a ride.

''Give me one good reason why I should get into a car with you,'' she demanded, thoroughly confused.

''One, you need a mechanic and I have a car phone—''

''I don't live far from here. I'll call him from home.''

''You'll still need transportation to get there and I don't see a cab in the vicinity. Two, you're soaked. And three...'' He found the words hard to get out, but he did owe her this much. ''I'd like to apologize.''

''Apologize?'' she echoed. ''Pardon me, but I don't believe I heard that right. Would you repeat—''

''You heard me,'' he snapped as the driver behind him honked. ''I'm sorry for the pass. Now, will you either get in or close the damn door so I can be on my way?''

She looked from him to her clothes and back again. Could she safely take his offer of a ride at face value? As he'd pointed out, she really didn't have any other option. She was wet and getting wetter, the rain was cold, the next bus wouldn't come for another hour and as he'd said, there wasn't a cab in sight.

''I'll ruin the upholstery,'' she said slowly.

Drew sighed impatiently. ''It's leather. Comes from cows. Cows have been known to stand out in the rain for days, maybe even weeks, without ruining their hides." The car behind him honked again. "Will you please get in?"

She eyed him skeptically as she complied with his request. "An apology and a 'please' in the same conversation. Are you sure you're the real Drew Casteel?"

He wouldn't be baited, he fumed, gripping the steering wheel. His errant thoughts, though, produced images of other things to do with his hands. Things that involved him and her and no clothing. He felt his body tighten.

"Which way?" he asked brusquely.

"Left at the light, straight six blocks, then right."

As he wove through the crush of the Plaza's evening traffic, Laine tried to sort through her conflicting thoughts. She wasn't happy with her own lack of control—the way her senses had gone crazy for the brief moment she was in his arms.

The big-bucks question was, *What was she doing in his car?* She'd left him tied to that file cabinet, livid over his caveman tactics, calling him every name she could think of, and wishing on him the worst case of backache ever documented in medical history.

Her car's failure to start hadn't improved her mood, but as she'd stood in the rain, the consequences of leaving Drew bound to the file cabinet had hit her. Nothing could have made her go back and release him, but she'd figured she would be job hunting in the morning.

Arthur would help her find a new job, but Drew, no matter how irritating his manner, would come first. He was family. While family ties hadn't counted for anything in her own situation, she'd heard the pride in Arthur's voice whenever he'd spoken about "my sister's boy, Drew." He would stick by his nephew.

Oh, well. She'd been in tight jams before and she'd be in tight jams again. In the meantime, she couldn't make matters much worse by satisfying her curiosity.

"Why the kiss?" she asked cautiously.

Drew had wondered the same thing while he'd wrestled to get free of the drawer. It wouldn't do to tell her he'd felt the urge from his first glimpse of her. Nothing had squelched the impulse to find out what her mouth would feel like under his. If only he could explain his actions to himself.

For now, he decided his best bet was to provoke her. But he was learning that even when they fought, she was hard to resist. He enjoyed seeing the fire and fury brighten her eyes and there didn't seem to be a damned thing he could do about that.

"Your sass," he replied. "When a woman smarts off to a man, she's issuing a challenge."

Laine growled in frustration. "Some men just can't deal with a woman who says what she thinks." Her father and her ex-husband, for two. "Turn left at the stop sign. It's the third duplex on the left."

Only he could turn something as rare and wonderful as that kiss into nothing more than a man showing a woman who was boss. Hadn't he felt any of the emotions, any of the wonder, that had swamped her? Why was it the one time she met someone who could awaken her senses, he was a throwback to earlier times?

Drew pulled into the driveway and Laine opened her door to make her getaway as quickly as possible. Her feet had no sooner hit the pavement than a high-pitched scream carried from the house to the blue coupe.

"Oh, not again." Laine sprinted from the car.

Instinctively, Drew shut off the engine and rushed into the house after her. A stout, gray-haired woman stood on a lumpy-looking beige sofa, her dark eyes filled with sheer fright. None of the furniture was overturned, nothing littered the worn carpet. So what was wrong?

"Where is he?" Laine growled.

Drew braced to fight him, whoever he was. No man had a right to terrorize a woman. The lady on the sofa pointed to an old Victrola cabinet against a wall beside the stairs. A young boy of nine or ten dashed down the stairs and dropped to his knees in front of the cabinet.

"Cody Aaron Sullivan." Laine glared at the boy as she knelt on the other side. When she bent forward to peer under the Victrola, the sight of her derriere was very distracting. "Put the shoe box on the other side," she instructed the boy.

He moved to her left. "Ready."

Taking a deep breath, she swept her arm under the antique's wooden legs. "Go, you slimy, scaly, slithering excuse for a pet."

"Name-calling's not nice," the boy retorted indignantly as he adjusted the box. Just when it appeared they had everything under control, he shouted, "Watch out!"

Laine jumped back with a gasp. The kid scrambled to catch the small thing that darted out from under the Victrola.

The old woman on the couch let out a scream that could shatter glass. Mouth agape, she pointed to Drew's pant leg. He looked down. A large brown-striped lizard clung to the fabric for dear life.

"Don't move a muscle," she muttered through clenched teeth as she stared at the creature.

In her tawny eyes was a determination to do her duty, no matter how distasteful the task. And Drew could tell by the wrinkle of her pert nose that this task was very unpleasant.

He held up a hand to stop her. The lizard was perfectly still, its attention focused on its two hunters. Drew bent down and captured the critter.

The boy applauded. The old woman sank onto the sofa cushions and made the Sign of the Cross. Laine's breath rushed out in relief.

"I'm sorry, Mom," the boy said.

Mom? Drew's mind raced. Laine had a son? She was married. No wonder the pass had angered her. But why didn't she wear a wedding ring? Where was her husband, and where did Arthur fit into this picture?

"Where was the encyclopedia this time?" she asked sternly.

The boy swallowed. "I needed that volume for my homework. Guess I forgot to put it back on the cage."

"One of the other nineteen books in the set would have held that cage lid down just as well."

"I didn't think of it," he said meekly. "Sorry."

Laine pushed her wet hair back from her forehead and sighed. "All right. Put Houdini back in captivity where he belongs while I take Consuelo home."

"Won't you need transportation?" Drew asked, hanging on to the wiggly creature in his hand.

"She rents the other half of the duplex. She comes over after school to stay with Cody." She helped the heavyset woman to her feet. "I'll get you home and start a pot of tea, Consuelo. How does that sound?"

"Very nice, Laine," Consuelo replied in a thick Spanish accent. "You know how I hate that...that thing."

"Yes, I know. Cody will put something on the lid and make sure this doesn't happen again. Ever! Otherwise

Houdini will go back to the wilds to fend for himself. Got that, Cody?'' She paused at the doorway to hear his answer.

"Yes, ma'am."

"Sounds like she's pretty steamed," Drew commented, studying the boy once the two women had left. The color of his hair and eyes, the shape of his mouth, left no doubt he was Laine's son. Even his shrug reminded Drew of hers.

"She cools off fast, though."

"Think she means what she said?"

"She means it." Cody opened the shoe box, then closed it. "The last time Mom caught him and tried to put him in the box, he jumped out before I got the lid on. Maybe if you could carry him upstairs to his cage..."

"No problem." Miniature monster in hand, Drew followed the kid upstairs to a room at one end of a short hall. The bed was made, the clothes picked up, the toys and books arranged in a set of tall bookshelves. In the far corner was a desk, a personal computer sitting on one side. In another corner was an aquarium. Cody removed the lid and Drew set the lizard inside.

"There. Mom will be glad he's back in his cage."

Drew chuckled. "I'm surprised she lets you keep him. From the look on her face, I figured she hated the thing."

"She does, but she's reasonable for a girl. She doesn't scream and freak out like Buzzie Baxter's mom."

Drew examined the screened lid. "A small piece of wood turned at the right angle might help hold this in place."

"Really? Could you... I mean..."

"It's okay. I can tell you what to get the next time your dad goes to the hardware store." Drew was fishing for information on Laine's situation, but right or wrong, he wanted to know.

"Mom's divorced."

Drew's brow arched at the succinct emotionless statement.

"Happened when I was little. I don't even remember my dad." Cody shrugged again, but Drew caught the hurt behind his words—the anger of a boy whose father hadn't spared a thought for him and what he was going through. Drew was surprised at the amount of empathy he felt for the boy. How well he himself knew the hurt of being deserted.

"Then I'll get what you need," he told Cody. "I'll bring it by tomorrow evening after work, and we'll fix it."

"Great. Thanks." The boy set another encyclopedia volume on the aquarium lid. "Oh, I'm Cody Sullivan."

"Drew Casteel."

"Arthur's nephew? Wow. He talks about you all the time. How you went to Texas A & M on a basketball scholarship and that you might give me a few pointers."

Before Drew could formulate a response, Laine called for Cody. The kid made a hasty dash down the stairs with Drew following more slowly, his mind scrambling to comprehend the boy's last words. How could it be that Arthur was singing his praises to others when the old man rarely complimented him to his face? Arthur hadn't even asked for his assistance with the construction company until the situation was serious.

"Mom!" Cody hollered out as his feet hit the bottom step. "Why didn't you tell me this was Drew? Mr. Casteel."

"Drew is fine," he said, standing beside the boy.

Laine caught Drew's smile, and focused on it, surprised to see it, fascinated by the way it deepened the lines around his eyes and brought out the faint cleft in his chin. He looked approachable, interesting, sexy as hell.

When she realized he and her son were watching her, she turned to Cody, banishing the dangerous thoughts from her mind.

"The orange bomb wouldn't start," she told him. "Would you call Bruce and see if he can check it out tonight? It's parked on the street in front of the office."

While Cody dialed, then asked for the mechanic, she slipped out of her wet jacket. When she glanced up, her gaze collided with Drew's. The warmth was back in his eyes, that frank appreciation she'd sensed in Arthur's office earlier that day. The heat reached out to her, chasing away the chill of her wet clothes.

His eyes caressed the shape of her breasts outlined by the damp silk blouse. She saw his hunger, felt it stir her own longings. She wanted him to kiss her again. The idea was ludicrous, completely without rhyme or reason, but she wanted it.

What was wrong with her? Why did that heat in his eyes short-circuit her thought processes? The man saw her as nothing more than a woman to control. She wouldn't be trapped in that kind of relationship again.

Cody hung up the phone, dragging Laine's mind away from its wayward course. "Bruce can't get to it until tomorrow, so we'll both be riding the bus. Can Drew stay for dinner?''

Laine's heartbeat stumbled at the thought of sitting across the table from him. At lunch, even through her outrage at the antiquated nonsense he spouted, she'd been very aware of him physically. Too aware. Now, after that kiss, she feared the intimacy of sharing a meal with him.

When in doubt, play it safe and avoid contact. She didn't need involvement with an unbending man who could turn her inside out with just one smoldering look.

"I can't stay," Drew said, sensing Laine's anxiety at Cody's question. He was tempted to stay, if only to see what would happen once they were alone again, but curiosity had gotten him into trouble once today. "I'd better be going, if everything's under control here."

Everything except her emotions, Laine thought as thunder echoed through the small duplex. On cue, the sky let loose a downpour to rival Niagara Falls. Cody dashed upstairs to shut off his computer and finish his homework before dinner. Laine glanced out the window, aware of Drew standing close behind her.

"It should let up soon if you want to wait," she heard herself say.

"I think I'll take you up on that."

She gave him a shaky smile and Drew couldn't tear his gaze away from her mouth. He didn't want to remember their kiss, but the memory refused to be banished. Logic insisted her wiles were blinding him to the dangers she represented. His hormones insisted he wanted her anyway. Rational thought reminded him of the cost of getting involved with the wrong woman. His need and careening emotions said damn the consequences.

When he pulled his gaze from hers, Laine released the breath she'd unconsciously held. He'd been on her case from the moment they met, then in the office he'd kissed her as if he'd had every right. And now she longed to experience the exquisite sensation of his kiss again. She was losing her mind. The man was ice one minute, fire the next—but what a fire.

"So how did you get free of that file cabinet?" she asked to break the awkward silence.

He smiled wryly. "The scissors on your desk."

"I'm surprised you could reach them from there."

"It wasn't easy."

As he explained the contortions he'd had to perform, her smile grew to a grin, then to full-fledged laughter. A musical sound. Enchanting. Captivating.

"How ingenious of you." She laughed again, then slowly sobered. "I'm sorry about the tie."

"I'll bet," he argued good-naturedly.

"Okay. Sort of sorry. It was a nice tie. Expensive, too, I'm sure. If I hadn't been so furious, I would have thought about that before I closed it in that drawer."

"Forget it." He reached behind her to part the curtains and peer out the window. The rain had slackened, but judging from the darkness of the clouds, more was on the way. "I'd better make a break for it now."

With a mixture of emotions, Laine watched him sprint out the door. Top on the list was surprise that he'd taken her setdown so good-naturedly. Then there was the way she'd responded to him, the way she'd felt the heat of his body beckon her to lean against him as he reached for the curtains. Then, there was relief that she still had a job, and dread that she would still have to work with Drew.

The man was a certifiable split-personality case. And she was in danger of losing her own sanity.

Chapter Four

Laine arched her back and stretched for the thousandth time today. At least it felt as if it had been a thousand times. She'd been typing for hours, the tedium broken by phone calls and requests from the staff for her attention.

The office was abuzz with news of the changes Drew was instituting. Laine was in a turmoil of her own, generated by the memory of his passionate kiss. She'd relived that moment over and over in her dreams, until she'd awakened aching for him and feeling lonelier than ever.

Drew had shown up on her doorstep this morning, looking sinfully tempting in his charcoal suit, offering to drive her to work. Arthur's orders, he informed her in a tone that dispelled any illusions she might have entertained.

Dr. Jekyll and Mr. Casteel. His mood changed from hot to cold as suddenly as the Kansas City weather. Today's forecast was brusque, hinting at possible storms on the horizon. The most imminent one centered around her young assistant.

A sharp word from Drew earlier today had sent Crissie cowering and not even a generous handful of the Tootsie Roll miniatures Laine kept in her desk drawer could coax the girl out of her terror.

At three-thirty, when Crissie threw up her lunch, Laine decided she would have to talk to him once the rest of the staff had gone for the day. She waited until the last person had clocked out, then gathered the forms she'd typed and headed for Arthur's office.

"Come," Drew said in answer to her quick rap on the door.

She walked inside, her steps momentarily faltering to see him seated behind the desk that belonged to her friend and mentor. She caught a flicker of heat in Drew's eyes as his gaze slowly skimmed over her. His frank appraisal rattled her composure, took the moment out of the business realm and made it decidedly personal. Too much so.

She had to regain her perspective.

"The personnel information you wanted," she said, holding out the papers.

She meant to simply hand them to him, but he stood, came around the desk and took them from her, his fingers grazing hers. Deliberately. She read that much in his gaze before the current of anticipation and excitement short-circuited her thinking.

Drew saw the precise moment the awareness shot through her. It was there in those expressive eyes of hers. Eyes a man could get lost in. The danger in that thought brought him to his senses.

He set the papers on his desk, took her arm and turned her toward the door. "I'll drive you home."

After a couple of steps she found her voice. "But... There's something I wanted to discuss with you."

"We'll talk in the car." Because if he stayed here with her, he would kiss her. Something he had no right to do.

He waited outside her office door while she gathered her things and turned out the lights, not quite daring to take any chances while there was a file cabinet within necktie distance.

Smiling to himself, he slid a hand into his jacket pocket and pulled out the section of the tie she'd locked in the drawer yesterday. He would remember that moment for a very long time. Remember her spirit. Remember the passion they'd unleashed for that too-brief kiss.

She came out of the office and stopped, her gaze immediately going to the scrap of tie he held. The memories were there for her, too. There for him to read in her guileless eyes.

"You should never play poker," he cautioned.

She blinked. "What?"

"Never mind." He stuffed the piece of paisley silk back into his pocket and reached for the three gallons of paint she held. "Mrs. Bradshaw was kind enough to bring me that piece of my tie this morning."

"Oh. Did she ask any questions?"

She was working to stifle a laugh, Drew realized. "Not a one. Just said she'd found it sticking out of the drawer and was bringing it to my attention because of the, uh, unusualness of the situation. And because it looked very similar in color and design to the tie I wore yesterday."

The tiny laugh finally escaped. "So you're off scot-free."

"Well, I didn't get the complete humiliation you had planned for me, though I richly deserved it for being such a jerk."

"If you feel so strongly about it, perhaps I could arrange something suitable—"

"Not on your life." With a chuckle of his own, he inclined his head toward the front door. "Lead the way," he told her.

Big mistake, he acknowledged as his attention zeroed in on the gentle sway of her slender hips. A sight to jump-start a fellow's libido. A lesser man would be panting with desire. He stopped just short of that, Drew decided as they walked to the car.

"'White exterior,'" he read from one of the paint cans as he placed them on the floor behind her seat. "What's it for?"

"The duplex," she said as he held the door for her. "Consuelo's brother owns the place, but he can't afford to hire someone to paint it, and he can't do it himself. So I'm helping out for a break on next month's rent."

"You're painting—" He closed the door once she was settled, and got in behind the wheel. "It's two stories tall."

"You noticed," Laine retorted, puzzled by the trace of alarm in his voice. If she didn't know better, she would swear he sounded downright protective. But she did know better. Didn't she? Still, as unlikely as his protectiveness was, she found herself wondering what it would be like to have him care.

"I'm not doing the whole place single-handedly," she told Drew as he pulled out of the garage. "Cody's helping. And Kyle."

"Kyle?" he asked with an edge of sharpness that confused her further.

"Kyle Rogers. He's one of the carpenters on Sam's crew." She decided to change the subject. "I wanted to talk to you about Crissie," she began, then noticed he'd turned left instead of right. "Home is the other way."

"I have to make a quick stop," he said in that brusque tone she was coming to know so well. "What about Crissie?"

"The gentle approach works best with her. She's young and very sensitive," Laine said in her best non-confrontational manner.

"If she can't take criticism, she'd better become damned good at what she does."

"She is good—"

"She filed the open Accounts Receivables in the Paid drawer and the Watkins contract was in the Watson folder. I hunted for it for over forty-five minutes."

"She made some mistakes today—"

"Right now, mistakes like losing Accounts Receivables and contracts could finish this company off."

He was right, Laine knew. "I promise to supervise her very closely if you will—"

"Not breathe fire around her?" he supplied.

Laine's eyes widened in horror. Then, to her amazement, one corner of his mouth twitched.

"I overheard her in the break room telling Sara that you call me Dragon Drew behind my back," he explained as he pulled into a parking space in front of the hardware store.

"I only said that to help her over her terror."

He chuckled. "So why is she so flustered by me and you're not?"

If he had any inkling what he did to her, she'd be in deep trouble, Laine thought. "Crissie is only nineteen. She's still finding her way."

"And you've found yours," he stated, shutting off the ignition. "You're very good at what you do."

"Thank you." *I think.* Who was this man in the car with her?

"I mean it. Arthur wouldn't have managed to stay afloat without your attention to detail and your skills at organization and dealing with people." He turned on the radio and opened the door. "Be right back."

He got out of the car, leaving the radio on and Laine speechless. She settled back and let the strains of a Mozart concerto surround her as she tried to sort through this latest exchange with the Master of Disguises. He'd been stern and distant all day, occasionally critical and always demanding. And now, just when she'd expected him to explode with righteous fury, he laughed. Then there was the unexpected compliment.

The man had her totally off-balance and thoroughly confused. But one thing was crystal clear. She could come to like this new side of him. Oh, yes...the charm, the gentleness and humor, wrapped in *the* most appealing male package she'd ever come across. She could easily become putty in his capable hands.

Something she wouldn't do if she was wise. At least not until she knew for sure just who Drew Casteel was. Besides, she reminded herself, his presence here was bound to be temporary. His home and business were in Dallas. One day he would go back to all he'd left behind.

On that note, Drew returned, opened the car door to put a small sack in the back seat, then slid in behind the wheel.

"About Crissie," he said as he pulled the Mercedes onto the busy street. "It's my understanding she's with the company on a temporary basis."

"She goes away to college this fall."

He nodded. "I can see the value of help over the summer, someone to pick up the slack during the busy season."

"But?" Laine prompted.

"We have to spend our payroll dollars carefully. The company can't afford to take in strays."

"I was a stray once myself."

"One with potential."

"Crissie has potential. It's just hidden under all that uncertain self-assurance."

He chuckled slightly. "Well hidden. But I'll trust your judgment for now."

Laine nodded, grateful for that trust, convinced it wasn't something he gave easily, or to everyone he came across. That he gave it now meant a lot.

She was still marveling at that when he pulled up in front of her duplex. Cody was shooting baskets, so Drew parked in the street. When Cody spotted the Mercedes, he ran up and opened Laine's door. He caught sight of the paint cans and groaned.

"Isn't it supposed to rain again?" he asked hopefully.

"This is supposed to be a totally dry weekend," Laine insisted. "The first one in two months and we're going to take advantage of it."

Cody grumbled some more, then brightened as Drew handed him the sack from the hardware store. "Hey, is this the stuff to fix the cage?" he asked.

"Cage?" Laine's eyes widened suddenly. "If that creature has gotten loose again . . ."

Drew chuckled. She was afraid of a little lizard she could squash with one foot. Yet in spite of that fear, she allowed Cody to keep the pet. Drew admired her spunk.

"We're going to make the aquarium escape-proof," he said, flashing a mischievous grin. "But maybe you want to stand guard over him while we work on the lid."

Her answer was immediate. "I don't think so. You guys are on your own. Where's Consuelo, Cody? I'll walk her home."

"In the kitchen."

Drew watched her walk up to the house, her shoulders sagging. He doubted she was aware he could read her weariness. Knowing her, she wouldn't want to show any weakness around him. Though that shouldn't bother him, it did. His earlier antagonism nagged at his conscience. Surprisingly, he longed to hold her, and tell her she wouldn't have to worry ever again. But he didn't have that right.

He waited until he and Cody were upstairs, then decided there was one thing he could do to help her out.

"Do you and your mom like pizza?" he asked as Cody dropped onto the edge of the bed and made room for Drew to sit.

"Yeah." Cody's dark eyes sparkled with enthusiasm. "Antonio's. With everything. Isn't Mrs. Jenkins cooking tonight?"

Drew frowned. "Mrs. Jenkins?"

"Yeah. We always go over to Arthur's on Friday night."

A fact he hadn't known until now. Another example of the lack of communication between him and his uncle, Drew thought. "He's not up to company tonight."

Cody's expression changed to concern—the way Laine's had when she'd walked into the office and found Arthur in distress. The boy had obviously inherited a good share of his mother's tendency to take care of the people close to her.

"What's wrong with him?" the kid asked.

"He overdid it yesterday, that's all. Dr. Manning wants him to rest over the weekend." Noting the boy's relief at the news, Drew dumped the sack's contents onto Cody's bed. "Do you know the pizza-delivery number?"

"By heart."

"Then order a large and you can have the leftovers tomorrow. Is there a phone up here? I want to surprise your mom."

Cody's eyes came alive with excitement. "Awesome. She loves surprises. Good surprises, not bad ones. Those make her worry. She thinks I can't tell, but I can. Even when she tries real hard to hide it."

Drew was getting a very definite picture here. Circumstances had changed the boy into a young man at an early age. Drew knew what it was to have your childhood snatched from you. He felt a connection to Laine's son—something unusual for him. Letting people get close was too risky.

"Come on," the boy said, jumping to his feet. "We can use the phone in Mom's sewing room."

Sewing room? Drew's silent query was answered when Cody opened the bedroom door across the hall. Patterns spilled out of an open dresser drawer and material was stacked on the cutting table along the far wall.

A sewing machine sat in front of the window. The soft fabric draped over it was a muted flowered print, and the pattern envelope on top of the material showed a thin-strapped sundress.

While Cody dialed the phone number, Drew's mind conjured up an image of Laine wearing the finished dress. The bodice would hug her firm, rounded breasts. The narrow waist would fit snugly, then flare gently at her hips. The skirt would follow the contours of her sexy derriere and the back's modest plunge would display a tantalizing amount of smooth, creamy skin.

She would be a vision. He pictured them dancing. A slow dance. She would be in his arms, the gold lights in her eyes warm, inviting, entrancing. He would hold her close, so close any other man around would know he was staking his claim on her. She would be all softness and feminine curves . . .

"Done," Cody said, hanging up the phone.

Drew's fantasy evaporated, but it wasn't gone forever. The dream was filed away in his consciousness, ready to be recalled when he was alone. If only it were wise to try to turn the dream into reality. He wanted her, but being with her would involve so many risks. He had an uncomfortable feeling she would change his life.

Still, there was a lure here that went far beyond sexual desire. The lure of hearth and home. Of warmth and caring he hadn't felt in a very long time. With Laine and her son, that temptation was stronger than ever. If only he could be sure it wouldn't vanish when he reached for it. . . .

"Let's see what we can do to keep Houdini where he belongs," Drew said, surprising himself with how right it felt to drape his arm over Cody's shoulder, surprised at how easily the boy accepted the gesture.

Back in Cody's room, Drew sat on the edge of the bed and picked up one of the wedge-shaped pieces of wood.

"Arthur said you held the record for most number of points scored in one game when you were at A & M," Cody said, plopping down beside him on the mattress. "For two years running."

Drew nodded, uncertain how to handle the boy's obvious admiration. This was different from Fred Fleming's praise of his business acumen. It shouldn't mean more to him, but it did. A lot more.

"Wow," Cody continued. "The record. For two years. That's really something."

But it hadn't meant much then, because there'd been no one to celebrate with him. His dad, as always, had been busy closing a merger deal and Arthur had been a long-distance phone call away—a call Drew hadn't bothered to make.

"Got a hammer?" he asked, smiling as the kid raced out of the room and returned in two minutes flat with the tool.

"So how'd you do it?" Cody asked breathlessly. "Set the record, I mean."

"Practice."

"Practice? That's it?"

Drew looked up from the wooden wedge he held. "That's the secret. What did you expect?" he asked gently.

Cody shrugged. "I don't know. Arthur says you were born with a gift for basketball. I'm so clumsy sometimes...."

Drew heard the frustration and remembered the awkwardness that came with rapid growth spurts. It wasn't any easier for Cody than it had been for him.

"Uncle Arthur has forgotten that I was pretty clumsy, too," he told Cody.

"*You* were? Really?" the boy asked skeptically.

"Honestly. Especially when things got intense. I blew a lot of games when I was your age. I had to practice myself out of my clumsiness."

There hadn't been anything else for him to do, those long and lonely days after his mother's death. He'd desperately needed to be part of some group—the team. Then, once on the team, he'd needed to excel, hoping to catch his father's or his uncle's notice. So he'd struggled to be the best. The very best.

"How come you quit basketball?" Cody asked. "Arthur said you had three offers to play pro after college."

"Because as good as I might have been, there were plenty of other guys out there who were even better." And he wouldn't compete where he didn't have a chance of coming out on top of the heap.

The kid's brow furrowed in thought. "But Mom says it doesn't matter if you're the best as long as you're the best you can be."

Did the boy realize how lucky he was to have such unconditional love and support from his mother? Could he imagine what a struggle it was to go through the childhood years without it? To go through almost your entire life without it?

"She's right. But I had to learn that the hard way." Eager to change the subject, he walked over to the lizard's cage. "So how did you end up with Houdini for a pet?"

"He belonged to my friend Buzzie Baxter, but his mom kept freaking out whenever he got loose. She couldn't eat or sleep, and she wouldn't open a cabinet or closet door 'cáuse she was scared he was going to jump out at her. So Buzzie's dad made him get rid of Houdini."

"And your mom let you take him," Drew said, still amazed that she had. "How did you get her to agree to the deal?"

The boy grinned impishly. "I told her that if Buzzie had to let it loose, a cat or a dog would get it and it would die a cruel and inhumane death. That's all it took."

So Laine truly did have a soft heart. He'd begun to suspect as much by the end of their first day together. Seeing her with Arthur and his staff, with Crissie, with Cody and the lizard, Drew had completely discarded the notion that she might be embezzling company funds. She was the kind of woman who took in strays, who nurtured. She reminded a man there was a gentler side to life, a side to be treasured.

But that gentler side was not for him. Each time he reached for it, fate slapped his hand away.

He turned his attention to Cody and his pet's quarters, showing the boy how to nail the wedge to the wooden lid to make it fit tightly while Cody made sure the lizard stayed inside.

"So where'd you learn stuff like fixing this?" Cody asked as he tested the tightness of the lid's fit.

"Summers in high school and college, I worked as a laborer for Arthur. You keep your eyes and ears open, you learn all kinds of things."

Cody chuckled. "Buzzie's mom says the only thing construction people can teach you is how to be vulgar."

"Arthur's been a construction worker all his life and he's never vulgar in front of a woman."

"That's what Mom says." Cody smiled up at him. "I'll bet it was really awesome to have Arthur for an uncle when you were growing up."

Drew nodded and forced a smile for Cody's benefit. It had been great at first, but everything had come to an end when they buried Drew's mother. He wouldn't relive the empty years that followed for anything. But how could he explain the desolation he'd felt?

Cody wouldn't understand. He couldn't. His childhood years seemed to be all they should be for a boy his age—even without his father's presence. That was certainly Laine's influence. She brought sunshine and smiles. All the things that made life seem full and happy.

"Mom's back," Cody said as a door downstairs opened and closed. "Are you staying for dinner?" he asked hopefully.

Drew didn't think it was wise to stay. He needed time to get his thoughts sorted out and his emotions under control before he spent an evening with Laine and her son.

"Another time, maybe." When the boy looked disappointed, Drew ruffled his hair. "Promise. We'll shoot some baskets." He reached into his pocket and pulled out a twenty-dollar bill. "For the pizza. Now, I'd better get out of here before the surprise comes."

He was learning that Laine was pretty independent. He wasn't sure how she would react to the pizza and he wasn't taking any chances.

Chapter Five

He'd been right to tell Cody he couldn't stay, Drew thought when Laine smiled up at him as he came down the stairs. The gentle warmth in her gaze was entirely too inviting.

She'd changed into jeans and an Earth Day T-shirt. In the casual clothes she looked every bit as enticing as she would in the sundress Drew had envisioned her wearing. She sat on the couch, socks in her hand, a pair of worn sneakers on the floor in front of her bare feet. Her ankles were slim, her toes delicate, dainty.

Funny, he'd never thought of feet as being particularly attractive, or appealing. But everything about Laine was alluring. Why couldn't he resist her appeal, enjoy it and still stay emotionally detached as he had with the other women who had come and gone in his life?

She looked as though she didn't have the strength to

put on the socks and shoes, he realized. "You could go barefoot around the house."

"I want to check the garden," she said, slipping on her socks. "With the rain, the weeds grow like crazy."

"Garden?" he echoed inanely.

"Beans, peas, leaf lettuce, green onion, a few garlic plants, peppers, tomatoes. Even some sweet corn, though this is the first year I've ever tried that. We'll have to wait and see how it turns out."

He should have known she didn't do anything by halves, especially if it involved nurturing. Before he could stop himself, he was wondering what it would be like to stay here with her for a while. If only he weren't so afraid everything would come crashing down around him if he did.

"Isn't it a lot of work? Especially after putting in forty-plus hours a week at the office?" he asked.

She shrugged. "Some things are worth the effort. If everything I planted comes up, by the end of July we'll be swimming in produce."

Drew was sure it would all grow and thrive under her care. He could imagine her picking the produce, canning enough to last through the winter, sharing it with Arthur and the neighbors.

That's when it hit him again—it was time to go.

"See you Monday," he said, still not moving toward the door.

Laine nodded, puzzled by her illogical longing to have this man stay. To have him work beside her, sit beside her at the dinner table and share the day's events. To have him nearby during the night, holding her. Dangerous longings.

"I forgot to thank you for the ride today," she said to change the course of her thoughts. "It really beats waiting for the bus."

"No problem. Will your mechanic have your car ready this weekend?"

She sighed. "He hasn't called yet to say how extensive the repairs will be, which probably means fixing it will cost more than the car is worth. And speaking of fixing things, did you really fix the lid on that lizard's cage?"

One corner of his mouth turned up. "Houdini's name will no longer apply to him."

"Thank heaven. You don't know how much I appreciate that. Consuelo, too."

He smiled. "It was an easy fix. Cody's a great kid."

Why did that mean so much, coming from this man? Laine wondered. Why did it matter that he thought highly of her son? It didn't make sense, but that was the way it was. "All prejudice aside, I have to agree."

The doorbell rang just then and the object of their conversation tore down the stairs, shouting, "I'll get it!"

"That's my cue to leave," Drew said, edging toward the door.

Making a suspiciously hasty getaway, he ducked out of the house and dashed to his car. Cody had transacted his business with the person at the door and was setting a pizza box on the table before Laine realized what had happened.

She stared at the box while her son set two plates on the table. "Pizza?" she asked.

"Drew wanted to surprise you. Wasn't that neat of him?"

"Yeah," Laine said uncertainly. She thought about his chauffeuring her to and from work, about his helping Cody with the cage lid. Now the pizza. He must have sensed she was too exhausted to cook dinner.

None of the above fit with the cold man who, up until now, had arrogantly issued orders to her. A dragon didn't suddenly stop breathing fire down a girl's neck, then cozy up to her. Not without an ulterior motive.

It would be so nice to think he might care for her; so dangerous to give in to the longings stirred by his occasional warm smiles and infrequent sympathetic looks. Was the pizza just a thoughtful gesture, or another way of showing his dominance?

"He ordered it just the way you like it," Cody said, pulling out one thick, gooey, cheese-and-toppings-covered slice and putting it on her plate.

Laine smiled to herself. "I imagine he had a little help in knowing just how I like my pizza."

"Okay. I helped," Cody admitted. "But the idea was all his. Dig in," he commanded around the mouthful he was trying to chew.

"Don't devour," she scolded gently. "There's plenty to go around."

"Sorry," he barely managed.

"Didn't you ask Drew to stay?"

Cody nodded, chewed rapidly, then swallowed. "He said he'd stay another time."

Which meant she wasn't off the hook yet, she thought with a sigh.

Through the rest of dinner, then as she and Cody washed the dishes, Laine continued to ponder the reason for Drew's changed manner. This warm and caring side of him was such a surprise. Pleasant as it was, she was afraid to trust that it would last. Afraid to trust that all was as innocent as it seemed on the surface.

When the last dish was put away, she still had no answer. It was as if she was trying to assemble a jigsaw while he kept scrambling the puzzle pieces, she thought as she folded the laundry. She had decided to leave the garden for tomorrow and call it an early night when the doorbell rang.

Dennis stood on the threshold, cap in his thick hand. "Nothing's wrong," he hastened to assure Laine. "It's just..."

She gestured for him to come inside. "Just what, Dennis?"

"Well, Mr. Masters was pretty put out that you and Cody weren't there for dinner like always."

"I thought it might be best to give him some time alone with Drew." And she'd been afraid she would be barging in where Drew didn't want her. She'd noticed how his warm looks became dark scowls whenever Arthur's name was mentioned in connection with hers.

Dennis ran a finger under his collar. "They're fighting, Miss Laine."

"Arthur and Drew? Arthur shouldn't be upset—"

"Yes , ma'am. I know. I tried to tell him, but he just told me to get you and Cody over to the house pronto."

A summons if ever she'd heard one. She called to Cody and rushed him into the Lincoln, explaining that Arthur was cranky and demanding their company.

Drew was aware his uncle should be kept calm, Laine knew. But Arthur could be difficult when he didn't get his way, and his confinement would make him even testier.

Fifteen minutes later, Dennis pulled into the semicircular drive and took the cutoff that led to the garage at the rear of the house. Drew was there in front of the garage, shooting baskets, putting tremendous energy into each shot.

It was obvious why he'd won the basketball scholarship, Laine thought, admiring his grace and agility. His tanned skin glistened with a fine sheen of honest sweat. His muscles bunched and flexed with his fluid movements. His soaked T-shirt was plastered to his broad back, showing off his strength and virility. She remembered what it had been like to be held by him, imagined what it would be like to be loved by him.

"Mom," Cody said excitedly, "do you think Arthur would mind if I shot baskets with Drew until dark? He said I should ask Drew to give me some pointers, remember? So I asked and Drew said he would."

"Good idea," she replied.

Drew was clearly working off steam. Cody could keep him occupied while she found out what was bothering Arthur. The man had to take care of himself and somehow she had to make him see reason. She found the patient in bed, pointing the remote control at the TV screen and angrily switching the channels.

"Not a damned thing worth watching," he complained to Emma Jenkins, his tone testier than Laine had expected.

"You're not giving the shows a chance," the housekeeper said from the wing chair beside the bed.

Laine walked into the room. "Hi," she said to Arthur, getting only a scowl for an answer. She turned to Emma. "Where's the nurse?"

"Taking a much-needed break," the housekeeper said with a heavy sigh. "She'll be back in time to give him his next tranquilizer."

Arthur swore. "Everyone's shoving pills down my throat. Emma, go away and leave us alone."

Emma wasted no time leaving her cranky patient.

"So," Arthur demanded, "just what the hell has he been doing to you?"

"Now, Arthur, calm down," Laine said firmly as she sat in the chair Emma had vacated.

Arthur's scowl only darkened. "Not until you tell me what that nephew of mine has been doing to you."

Driving her crazy with never knowing what to expect from him. Making her wonder for the first time since her divorce what it would be like to share her life with someone. Turning her inside out with wanting him. But those were things she wouldn't admit aloud.

"Why do you think Drew's done anything to me?" she asked instead.

"Because you weren't here last night, or tonight—you and Cody haven't missed a Friday night in over a year."

"I don't have a car—"

"Dennis will come and get you and take you anywhere you want to go."

"Thank you, but I was tired tonight—"

"That's never stopped you before."

She was beginning to understand where Drew came by his annoying habit of not letting a person finish a sentence. "I also thought you and Drew could use some time together."

Arthur eyed her sharply. "The truth?"

Partly, she said silently. She couldn't explain that she'd feared Drew would perceive her visit as intrusive. That would upset Arthur even more. "When he's come to town in the past, you've always shuffled him off to a hotel."

"I didn't want to tie him down. He grew up in Kansas City. And he's single. I thought he'd like time to get reacquainted with his old friends and some privacy to entertain."

She took a deep breath to dispel the unreasonable rush of jealousy she felt at the thought of Drew with another woman. "Did you ever ask him if that's what he wanted?"

"Why should I have to ask?" the older man snapped.

"I think you might be surprised by the answer."

Arthur leaned up on one elbow to peer intently at her. "What do you mean?"

She shouldn't care about Drew's relationship with his uncle, she told herself. He wouldn't appreciate her interference at all. Still, she knew what it was like to have a family and lose it. So did he. Cody was all she had now, and he was the most precious thing in her life. Drew had Arthur, but the more time she spent with the two men, the more she wondered if either had ever told the other how much he valued their relationship.

But she could be way off base, thinking Drew wanted a closer relationship with his uncle. Where he and his feelings were concerned, she was operating in the dark.

"Well?" Arthur prompted.

There was no way out of this but to speak her mind. "I'm saying you shouldn't presume to know what someone else is thinking. Isn't that what you've always told me?"

"Humph. I know what I saw yesterday in my office. I may have been hurting and scared, but I didn't miss his coldness toward you. And then when I called today, Mrs. Bradshaw mentioned that things were tense at the office with him there. I just don't understand that boy."

"Drew is hardly a boy." He was all man, and if anyone needed proof, it was in the way he brought her senses to life. Legs stretched out in front of her, Laine studied her shoes while she thought over what she could tell Arthur to make him rest easier about the office situation. "He and I just need to learn how to work together."

"I guess that's one explanation," Arthur conceded.

"What's the other?" she asked, knowing there was more on the older man's mind and that he wouldn't rest until he'd gotten all he wanted off his chest.

"That when he wants to be, he's as cold as the iceberg that sank the *Titanic*. I've seen it, and I saw him giving you a taste of it."

"Then it's my business. You've always backed me up, but you've made me fight my own battles, right?"

His barely audible mumble told Laine she'd made her point.

"So what were you two fighting about?" she asked cautiously, hoping she wouldn't upset him further.

"Ha. That's my battle and my business. Go find Cody," he commanded. "I want to find out what grade he's going to get in math."

One thing was for certain, Drew acknowledged as he watched Cody line up his next shot. No one could stay in a rage around this kid. The boy's cheerful spirit simply did not allow it.

Arthur had been furious when he had told him Laine and Cody weren't coming tonight, demanding to know why, delivering a tirade on Drew's heavy-handed ways, declaring Drew had no right to restructure his uncle's personal life—especially if that meant keeping him from the people he cared about.

Drew would have argued that Arthur needed his rest, but he'd been too concerned about his uncle's condition to protest. And too hurt to realize how important Cody and Laine were to the old man and how little his own presence meant.

"See, I'll never get the hang of this!" Cody fumed as his shot went wide. "I can't get my wrist to stay straight."

"I think I have a solution," Drew said, studying the boy's slender frame. Like Drew himself at nine years old, Cody was all height and little bulk. "Weights."

"Yeah," he said with his trademark enthusiasm. "But Mom says I'm too young." He planted his hands on his hips, a perfect parody of his mother. "'If you want to work out'," he mimicked, "'you can start by mowing the yard. Or whatever else needs to be done,'" he finished, rolling his eyes.

Drew laughed. "She does need your help around the house, but as long as you agree to do your chores, I'll talk to her, see if I can't get her to change her mind."

"Awesome!"

"We won't call it working out, though."

"Just not to her, anyways."

"Right," Drew agreed. A boy needed to be able to brag to his friends a bit. "We'll start with some hand weights and see how that goes over. I'll tell her you're working on strength in your arms, demonstrate how much it will help you." Drew took aim, then sent the ball arcing into the air. It sailed through the net with a quiet woosh. "Like that. Then maybe we can talk her into karate for control."

"Karate! Wait till I tell Buzzie. He'll go absolutely crazy!"

"First things first," Drew cautioned. "We've got to take it one step at a time. If we rush her, she's apt to turn down the whole idea."

"Oh, you can't let her do that. Tell me what we have to do."

Drew wasn't sure he should be aiding and abetting this way, but he could tell that Laine's nurturing, wonderful as it was, might extend to protectiveness. And that could be very confining to a young boy.

"We have to be patient. First we approach her about the weights. Then in a month or two, when she starts to see the improvement, I could start casually mentioning karate and the control it would give you."

"Perfect. I'll be back from SPACE CAMP by then."

"SPACE CAMP?"

"Yeah. It's really cool. You get to learn how to be a real astronaut and everything. This will be my second year."

"Okay, then, when you get back, we'll talk to her about karate."

"But can you tell her about the weights now?" Cody asked.

"Now?" He'd thought he might take her out to dinner, somewhere quiet, maybe romantic. Obviously he hadn't counted on Cody's impatience.

"Yeah, now. Here she comes. Hi, Mom. Bye, Mom. I'm going in to check on Arthur." Before either adult could respond, they heard the soft slam of the kitchen door close behind Cody.

Laine stared at the door thoughtfully. "He's awfully excited," she murmured.

Drew laughed. Nothing much got past her.

"In fact, watching you two out here a moment ago, I got the distinct sense of a conspiracy being hatched."

Poor Cody didn't stand a chance, Drew thought, taking a couple more shots. Laine waited with determined patience. Drew made one final basket, then decided to plunge in.

"It's like this. I was showing Cody how much a little muscle development in his upper arms would help him with his shots. I thought some hand weights—"

"Oh, no. I don't want him to get obsessed with this bulking-up stuff. If he wants to develop something, let him develop his mind."

"The two are not mutually exclusive." He held up a hand to prevent her instinctive protest. "And he's a long way from being obsessed with the idea. We're just talking about some hand weights he can use around the house."

"That sounds suspiciously like just the beginning. He's been wanting to work out—"

Drew chuckled. "Come on, Laine. To a nine-year-old, a couple of hand weights is working out. This is light-duty stuff here. Just a little something to help him develop a bit more power and control. Here, let me show you what a difference it can make."

Laine's breath caught as his arms encircled her. Sensations crowded in and rational thought halted abruptly. He turned her to face the goal and put the basketball in her hands. His body heat wrapped around her as he pulled her close until her shoulder blades pressed against his chest. His long, capable fingers closed around her hands and the dark hair on his arms brushed her skin, sending tiny shivers rushing along her nerve endings.

"There's a lot of arm and wrist action involved in basketball," Drew said when he could find his voice.

He should have known her nearness would play havoc with his equilibrium. Oh, man, he should have known. Holding her was exquisite torture, and he didn't want it to end.

"Be fluid," he told her, desperately trying to stick to the matter at hand. "Let me lead."

It took all his effort to concentrate on taking aim at the basket, but the movement of making the shot brought their bodies closer together. So close he could feel the outline of her curves. The breeze blew her sweet, tempting scent up to tickle his nose.

Stifling a groan, he made the shot, then turned her in his arms. Before the ball was halfway to the net, before he could think, he kissed her.

Laine stiffened as his hand splayed across her back, pressing her to him. She could not let this happen. Not again. But how could she stop him when this was where she wanted to be? Where she'd needed to be from the moment she spotted him in his sweat-dampened T-shirt.

His fingers caressed the sensitive skin at her nape, scattering what little resistance she hadn't managed to summon. She gave herself up to the thrill he sent rushing through her. He seemed to know exactly what she needed. He took greedily, yet gently, with passion and purpose, yet with infinite patience.

She savored this tenderness she found in him. It was a temptation all its own and every bit as powerful as his kiss. With a sigh, she wrapped her arms around him, tentatively exploring with her hands and fingertips the solid plane of his back.

He'd never been this close to insanity, Drew thought. Driven there by a desire more urgent and intense than he'd ever known before. He couldn't taste enough of her sweet mouth. Couldn't get enough of the feel of her hands on him. He wanted so much more. . . .

He urged her closer until her small breasts pressed against his chest. Her heat enveloped him, drove away reason, doubt and fear. No matter the danger, he had to have more. His hand slid lower, to cup her derriere and urge her closer still.

At his bold touch, Laine gasped, suddenly, finally coming to her senses. How could she have let herself get so out of control? She ached to have him show her how wonderful it could be between them. She'd given in to her own desires, and had reveled in his bold touch. Had wanted him to take her, then and there.

He had no right to haul her into his arms and kiss her senseless. Even if that was exactly what she wanted him to do. Breathing hard, she jerked free.

"Laine," Drew said, sounding as breathless as she felt. "I didn't mean for this to happen."

She understood. Desire had drowned out the voice of reason for her, too. "It can't happen again." It would be much too dangerous.

She turned toward the house to find Arthur there at the library's French doors, Cody standing behind his wheelchair. How much had the two seen?

"What's going on?" Arthur demanded, as Laine rushed into the library, Drew behind her. Arthur's eyes fastened darkly on Drew.

"I was coming to get Cody," Laine answered quickly, noting Arthur's glower and not wanting uncle and nephew to pick up their disagreement where they'd left off. "Find Dennis," she told her son. "It's time for us to go."

The boy knew when not to argue with his mother. In a matter of minutes, he called down the hall to tell her Dennis was ready to drive them home.

Feeling Arthur's scowl still on him, Drew followed Laine to the front door. She wanted him as much as he wanted her, he knew. What would it take to make her give in to that desire? What would happen to him if she did? Could he make love with her and remain untrapped by his emotions? Would she chew him up and spit him out as Caro had done?

Although that brief unpleasant trip down memory lane gave him pause, it didn't check his raging hormones. He had an uneasy feeling he would lose at love a second time around, just as he'd lost the first time.

Chapter Six

Saturday dawned sunny and pleasantly warm, as the weatherman had promised. Laine absently stirred a gallon of paint, chewing a Tootsie Roll while she thought over all that had happened last night.

Starting with the way Drew had approached her on Cody's behalf, trying to sway her to their side of the argument on weights. In a way it was cute, the two of them conspiring against her, so to speak. There was something touching about her son turning to him and about Drew's willingness to take up his cause.

What was Drew's interest in the matter, though? It all seemed innocent enough, but... She knew so little about the man.

Except where his passion was concerned. She knew the wonder of being in his arms. Knew the fires he could ignite with just a kiss. Knew how it felt to have her body come alive and beg for his touch.

Knew, also, the foolishness of wanting what was all wrong for her.

She jumped when someone touched her shoulder.

Startled, Kyle pulled his hand away. "Hey, what's with you this morning?"

"Nothing."

"Don't give me that. I said three times the paint has been mixed enough and you keep right on stirring." He looked around as a car pulled into the driveway. A blue Mercedes. His eyes widened in surprise as Drew got out. "What's the new boss doing here? Looks like he's here to paint, too."

He couldn't be. But Laine glanced over Drew's worn gray T-shirt and faded jeans and had to agree with Kyle. She popped another Tootsie Roll into her mouth, then went back to stirring paint, her hand clenched around the stir-stick as she fought to control her runaway longings for the man walking toward her.

"Good day for painting," Drew said, striding into the garage.

He looked much too ruggedly male, much too tempting to her still-chaotic emotions. She couldn't handle this. Before she could think of what to say to send him on his way, Cody spotted him and gave a whoop of joy.

"Are you going to help us paint?" he asked.

Drew held up a sack from the hardware store. "I bought extra brushes and a scraper." He smiled at Laine. "In case you didn't have enough to go around."

"Look," she said, straightening, trying in vain to ignore the crazy things his devilish grin did to her insides. "I'm sure you must have other things to do. Arthur is probably bored—"

His grin widened. "Actually, when I told him you planned on painting this place practically by yourself—"

"I told you yesterday that Kyle and Cody would be helping," she protested.

"Yes, well, I didn't tell him that much."

She planted one hand on her hip. "Didn't tell him?"

"He wouldn't give me the chance. I barely got out your name and the word *paint* before he went ballistic. Demanded I get over here ASAP and lend a hand."

Drew didn't add that the old man's orders suited his plans perfectly. He'd made up his mind last night that he was going to spend a lot of time with Laine—enough time to get her out of his system. He'd long since quit believing in love, but he needed to get his feelings, his need, for this woman in line, and he couldn't think how else to do it.

"That sounds like Arthur," Kyle said. "Always looking after Laine. Well, I for one am glad for the extra hand."

"Me, too," Cody insisted earnestly.

Laine was the only one who had no comment, Drew noted with a large degree of satisfaction. He was getting under her skin, just the way she'd done with him, and that was precisely where he intended to stay.

"So, let's get this show on the road." He gestured to Kyle. "We can start at the corner—you and Cody on the back of the house and Laine and I will take this side."

This day was not supposed to turn out this way, Laine thought as they got down to business. Drew had expertly maneuvered things so the two teams got farther and farther apart as the work progressed. Then, he whistled while he worked. After a while, Laine found herself focusing on the melodious sound and recognizing bits of the classical tune she'd heard on his car stereo. Between tunes, he was surprisingly talkative.

She tried to ignore the thrill of working with him. His manner this morning—comfortable and companionable—was a lure all on its own. Add to that the memory of their brief moment of passion last night.... How long had she wished for this type of relationship?

"Laine."

She laid down her brush and looked up at him, shielding her eyes from the late-morning sun, hoping her expression didn't betray her thoughts.

"I'm ready for more paint. Steady the ladder while I come down, would you?"

She watched him descend, unwillingly admiring the way his jeans hugged his hips. Once on the ground, he paused to pull off his shirt, revealing an expanse of well-defined chest covered with a mat of soft dark hair.

Laine had to stuff her hands in her pockets to keep from touching him. The longing to feel his skin under her palm was strong, alarming in its intensity. A male torso had never affected her this way. This was the wrong man, the wrong chest, the wrong feelings.

She shook her head to clear away the unwanted thoughts. But when she looked up and discovered he was doing his share of staring at the front of her sweat-dampened T-shirt, her errant thoughts refused to budge. There was a heat in his eyes to rival that racing through her bloodstream.

Drew raised his gaze to her face. Her eyes were wide, dark, hungry. He wanted to take her in his arms, press her slender frame to him, and kiss her again. The urge got more powerful each moment they were together. But this was not the time or place, he acknowledged with a sigh as Cody came around the side of the house.

Drew reached to touch her cheek, settling for that tiny contact. "You have paint here," he said, wiping the small smudge off her face. The soft texture of her skin only made it more difficult to resist his impulses.

Cody laughed as Drew rubbed at another spot of paint above her eyebrow. "Looks like Mom should have given herself the neatness lecture she gave me, huh?"

One corner of Drew's mouth twitched.

"Scram, both of you," she scolded with mock severity.

Drew dropped his arm over the boy's shoulder. "Come on, pal. Let's refill our buckets and get back to work."

Breathe normally, Laine commanded herself, drawing in a lungful of air when the pair walked away. She unwrapped another Tootsie Roll. The situation was more dangerous than she'd feared. Her hormones were getting out of hand at the mere sight of a little skin.

Well, not such a little amount, she mused, picking up her brush. His chest was broad, perfectly formed and thoroughly distracting. She put all her energy into work, trying to banish any stray, unwanted thoughts. But Drew's proximity made it impossible. As the day wore on, her irritation with the entire situation grew.

He should not be helping with the painting. She still owed him for the pizza and the rides to and from work, and now she owed him for today, as well. She didn't like the idea of being in his debt.

He should not be giving orders, arranging things so the two of them worked virtually alone. This was her house. She should be in charge and he shouldn't be here at all.

He should not be pleasant and so damned sexy, and she should not be enjoying his company. She shouldn't like listening to him whistle, shouldn't thrill to the sound of his voice and his husky laughter, shouldn't be driven to distraction at every glimpse of his bare chest and back.

The more she tried, and failed, to ignore his charm, the more annoyed she became—with herself, with him, with the house for needing to be painted.

When they finished for the day, Kyle announced he couldn't stay for dinner. Although Laine reminded him she'd promised to provide beer and all the enchiladas he could eat in exchange for the work, she couldn't change his mind. Drew offered to clean the brushes and stow the ladders in the garage so Kyle could be on his way. Then Mr. Helpful gallantly offered to stay for dinner, since Laine had planned for one extra anyway. What was she supposed to say to that?

He was proving to be a pro at creating problems for her. She would get through dinner then get him out of the house immediately afterward, before her wants and longings carried her into bed with him. When she turned around, he was spraying the garden hose over the brushes and paint buckets. His head was bent, but Laine thought she detected a satisfied gleam in his eyes.

He who laughs last, she muttered. She checked on the little bit of work Cody had left to finish on the other side of the house, then stalked back over to one of the ladders.

"Leave that," Drew ordered without glancing up. "I'll get it as soon as I've finished with these."

"I can manage." The sooner things were put away, the sooner she could start dinner, and the sooner she could get rid of his unsettling presence. Being near him all day was all her reeling senses could endure. She was perilously close to giving in to the desire to be in his arms again, to feel his lips pressed against hers, to experience the sensations he could bring to life.

All those feelings were out of line, she thought, watching him kneel down to rinse a bucket. She needed to have him gone, and to have him understand she wouldn't take orders from him outside the office.

"Laine," he growled when she reached for the ladder again. "Leave it. It's too heavy for you."

He obviously didn't know who he was talking to. She wasn't a weakling. She had learned to take care of herself.

She gripped the ladder. She'd only lifted it an inch off the ground when a spray of icy water hit the back of her bare legs beneath her jean shorts. She yelped. The ladder clattered to the ground, nearly taking her with it.

She turned to glare at Drew.

"That was to get your attention," he said, dropping the hose, then advancing toward her with long strides.

Her hands went to her hips. "I said I could manage—"

"And I said leave it."

She looked up into the determined expression of the man towering over her and decided there was no use arguing with him. She would have to get her point across another way. "Fine. You take the ladder and I'll clean the brushes."

"About time you got over your stubbornness," he muttered.

Fists clenched, Laine walked over to the buckets and brushes. The battle wasn't over yet, she vowed, picking up the hose. She waited until Drew had lifted the aluminum ladder, then aimed the frigid spray at his bare torso.

His curse was satisfyingly eloquent. He backed up two steps but couldn't dodge the stream of water directed at him. He stepped sideways, but she continued to pelt him. He took a step toward her, but she aimed the spray higher so the water blinded him and effectively cut off his sputtered commands for her to stop.

Savoring the taste of victory, she didn't see him make his move. Lightning fast, he dropped the ladder and lunged for her, catching her wrist. With one hand he took the hose out of her grip. With his other, he pulled her to his chest. Her breasts were pressed against his wet skin. Her T-shirt absorbed the cold moisture.

"Drew...I..." She pushed against his chest with her free hand.

"Oh, no, you don't," he said quietly. Too quietly. "You've been spoiling for a fight all afternoon, and unless I miss my guess, we're suffering from the same ailment...."

She gasped as his hand slid lower to cup the curve of her bottom. Don't let this happen again, logic warned. But you want this, desire pleaded. The war was waged in a heartbeat, and logic, the loser, was banished to some far reaches of her mind.

She welcomed his kiss. Ravenous, her senses drank in the tastes and textures. His beard stubble was rough against her cheek. His breath was warmer than the afternoon sun that beat down on them. His muscles were hard, pressed against the length of her.

She clung to him, lost in the onslaught of sensations more intense than any she'd ever known. Hot waves of desire crashed over her. Thought was impossible. She could only feel. And want.

She melted against him as he urged her closer still. Her breath caught when she realized he was very aroused. With that knowledge came a heady feeling of power she wanted to explore. She met the thrust of his tongue, surprised by her boldness, pleased when his arm tightened around her.

Drew couldn't get enough of her. She tasted of passion and the Tootsie Rolls she'd been eating a moment ago. He was on fire. Her unrestrained response was driving him over the edge of control, but he couldn't stop. Her fingers were splayed against his chest, but he wanted more skin-to-skin contact. He tugged at her outstretched wrist, needing to have her touch him, hold him.

What he received was a shower cold enough to take his breath away. The forgotten hose doused them both. Laine squealed, jumping out of his arms. Cody came around the corner of the house, saw his dripping mother and the garden hose Drew held.

"Water fight!" he shouted exuberantly.

Drew looked to Laine, his brow raised inquiringly. She shrugged. Taking that as permission, he turned the stream of water on Cody. The boy danced around the yard, but couldn't run away from the cold spray. When he caught his mom laughing, he ran behind her, begging for protection.

She straightened and stared at Drew, challenge gleaming in her eyes. Her T-shirt clung to her breasts, making him long to kiss the budding nipples that stood out in reaction to the wet cloth and the afternoon breeze, and the kiss they'd shared. God, how he wanted her.

He needed action to change the direction of his thoughts. When Cody peered over his mother's shoulder to holler, "Chicken!" and Laine added her, "Yeah, chicken!" to the taunt, Drew blasted the pair.

The two screamed in unison, clinging to each other, both slipping on the wet grass, each scrambling to use the other as a shield. They were laughing so hard they couldn't speak.

"Get him," Laine finally managed to gasp to her son. "Get Drew."

They charged at him, but he had the advantage. When Cody got close, Drew pelted him until he was forced to retreat. Laine was more persistent, but Drew easily held her at bay. Her warnings and threats to him were barely distinguishable through her laughter.

In their three-day acquaintance, Drew had seen many facets of her personality—the efficient office manager, the concerned friend, the firm and affectionate parent, and the passionate woman. But this glimpse of her, carefree and fun-loving as a child, captivated him. He didn't want this moment to end, but before long the exhausted pair had run to the other side of the house, out of range of the hose.

When they didn't return, he felt oddly bereft. He called to them, but there was no answer. He wanted the play to continue forever, even while he knew that was impossible. The screen door leading from the garage into the house banged shut.

It had been like that all his life—he was allowed a glimpse of true sharing, real caring, only to have the door slam shut in his face. He bent to rinse the bucket Cody had dropped.

A moment later he looked up and realized he'd been had. Cody charged him from the left, Laine from the right. He should have seen it coming, Drew thought wryly as he gave the fight his best. This divide-and-conquer tactic was one the two had used on the unsuspecting lizard.

Just like poor Houdini, he didn't stand a chance.
Laine lunged for the hose as Cody clipped him behind
the knees. He went sprawling on the wet grass, more
than willing to lose this fight. Laine gave a victorious
whoop as she wrestled the hose from his loose grip.

"Say your prayers, varmint," she warned just before the blast of cold water hit him.

She didn't let up until he was choking—with laughter as well as the volume of water that splashed off his
chest and into his mouth. When he finally managed to
shout his surrender, she allowed Cody to shut off the
water.

"We were awesome," he proclaimed loudly.

"Righteous." Laine raised her hand to give him five.

"Sneaky," Drew accused, grinning at the conspira-
tors.

"You thought we went inside," Cody stated. "Mom
said you would."

"So you're the one responsible for my defeat."
Drew's eyes narrowed on her. The soaked T-shirt clung
more provocatively than before, making it nearly impossible for him to think straight.

Laine caught the direction of his gaze and felt the
ache his kiss had started grow stronger. "Cody, help
Drew clean up out here. I'm going in to get dinner
ready."

Where had her resolve to get rid of Drew gone? She
showered and dressed, aware that she was now looking
forward to the rest of the evening with him.

She was asking for trouble with these feelings, she
admonished herself as she straightened the bathroom.
He was distractingly sexy and very charming when he
chose to be. But he was a man who kept his thoughts to
himself, one accustomed to keeping everyone else on the

outside. Getting involved with that kind of man had been a costly mistake. One she wouldn't repeat.

Laine strolled into the kitchen to find Drew hanging up the phone, a change of clothes clutched in his other hand, and Cody stepping out of his soggy, muddy sneakers.

"Drew and I weeded the garden while we were out there," he said, scooting past her. "And I'm headed for the shower right now," he added before she had to remind him.

Was that Drew's influence? she wondered. "Checking on Arthur?" she asked as she set a bowl of chopped lettuce on the counter.

"Emma says he's fine," Drew answered. "Um, Laine, why don't you let me take you and Cody out to dinner. You've got to be tired—"

"I'm fine and everything's ready. I just have to pop it into the oven. You can use the shower in the downstairs bath. It's through my bedroom."

He wanted to insist, but the determination in her gaze warned him to let the issue go. In her shower, he picked up her perfumed soap and sniffed its wildflower fragrance. If he used it, he would smell her scent all night long. It would be like lying next to her without being able to touch her. He wanted her like crazy as it was, and the added distraction would send him over the edge. He put the perfumed soap back in its dainty round dish and scrubbed himself with the deodorant bar.

What would it take to make Laine give in to her desire? What would happen to him if she did? He'd lost at love many times—his mother, his father, Arthur, Caro—and he was sure it would happen with Laine. And when the dust settled on his affair with her, picking up the pieces would be harder than ever.

Drew finished his shower, dressed in his fresh clothes, then went back into the kitchen. Cody was setting the table. Laine was bent over, checking something in the oven. The sight of her derriere held his attention more completely than any tricky business deal ever had. Odd, for someone who always gave business precedence over everything else. It was a clear warning to watch his step around her.

Then Cody spotted him. "Drew's here," he told his mother.

She straightened. Drew noted the brief flash of hunger in her eyes as her gaze skimmed over his khaki shorts and yellow knit shirt. "Dinner in about five minutes."

She wiped her hands on a striped apron that stated "Kiss the Cook" in bold black letters. Drew was tempted to obey the command, but instead settled for asking, "Anything I can do to help?"

She shook her head. "Would you like a beer while we wait for the enchiladas?"

"Sure. Cody, could you get it for me, please?" he asked, figuring he could spare her that much trouble at least.

"Great water fight," the boy said, handing Drew the bottle.

"Sure was."

The play had been exhilarating, stimulating, and had made him feel very close to mother and son. Made him feel like part of a family.

He'd had that once, before his mother had died in a boating accident and his father had become too involved in work to have time for him. He'd thought he had that with Arthur, but it, too, had vanished after his mother's death and he'd never had the nerve to tell his uncle how much he missed their former closeness. He'd thought he'd found that with Caro, but soon discovered all he had was fool's gold.

The kind of deep and lasting relationship he wanted eluded him every time. Would a relationship with Laine be as superficial and fleeting as the others in his life? Why did watching her and Cody make him realize how truly empty his life was? Why did he have the feeling he would always be a loner, always be on the outside looking in?

Cody talked through dinner, from the time Laine set the crisp fresh salad on the table until they'd consumed the last of the chicken enchiladas. When the final crumb had been devoured, Drew insisted he and Cody would do the dishes while Laine took a break. She resisted the idea, but surrendered when the phone rang and Cody told her Bruce wanted to speak to her.

From what Drew could gather, the mechanic estimated repairs to the Volvo at over fifteen hundred dollars, and he'd found another car. She hung up the phone and went to her desk in the living room. Drew could see her sitting there, scribbling on a scrap of paper and occasionally punching numbers into a hand calculator. She didn't seem happy with the figures it gave her. When the phone rang again, she pushed the calculator aside and reached for the receiver.

Cody beat her to it. "Mom!" he called out after a brief animated conversation with the person on the other end of the line. "Buzzie wants me to come over and see his new Nintendo game. Can I? We're done in the kitchen."

"I guess so. Just be—"

"Careful crossing the street and get home before dark. Will you be here when I get back?" he asked Drew.

He nodded, catching a flicker of alarm in Laine's eyes. Was she afraid to be alone with him? He needed to stay, Drew realized. He didn't know exactly what he wanted from her, other than to make love to her, but there was an excitement and a peacefulness in being with her. Dangerous feelings, but ones he wasn't ready to give up.

He got out the television listings, found a good movie on one of the channels, then settled back on the couch and invited her to sit beside him. She did, though with more than a little hesitation.

After a few minutes, he began to doubt the wisdom of his actions. Being this close to her and keeping his hands to himself required more willpower than he'd thought.

This attraction between them had been eating at him all day, all last night, ever since he'd first seen her. Their brief battle over the ladder had brought all his longings to the surface and he'd kissed her without thinking, without control. What would have happened if the cold water hadn't doused the fire she'd ignited?

After a while she sank back against the lumpy cushions, her legs curled up under her. Cody came home a little after nine, said a quick good-night, then disappeared upstairs.

"I should go, too," Drew suggested when she yawned.

"Stay and watch the ending," she said.

That was all the coaxing he needed, though he'd long ago lost track of the film's plot. Her nearness was too much of a distraction. He got them each a beer when the next set of commercials came on, and they sipped the cold brew while the rest of the movie played.

When it was over, he glanced down at Laine, prepared to say a reluctant goodbye. But she'd fallen asleep. He stared at her for a few moments, then carefully extracted the half-full bottle of beer from her hand. She breathed deeply, but didn't waken. Knowing he was only torturing himself, he eased her head against his shoulder. She snuggled against his side with a small sigh.

She was warm, small, and she fit perfectly next to him. A couple of times she moved slightly, but always to burrow closer. He sat like that for the better part of two hours, too lost in the enjoyment of having her this close to leave. For a short while he needed to pretend she belonged to him, that he belonged to her.

At midnight he knew he had to go before his control snapped. He sat up and shook her gently. She roused a little, only to unconsciously settle into his arms. Drew lifted her off the old couch and carried her into the bedroom. Her eyes opened as he lowered her to the bed.

"What—" Her voice caught as alertness returned.

"Go back to sleep," he said softly. "I'll lock up on my way out."

Gazing into her puzzled expression, he knew she was trying to work out what might have happened between them. He planted a tender kiss on her mouth. Her response was slow, but when it came, it took all of Drew's willpower not to climb into bed with her. He knew he could convince her to make love to him with very little effort, but when she gave herself to him, he needed her to be fully aware of what she was doing. It shouldn't matter, but it did. Very much.

"Good night, sweetheart," he said as he let himself out of her room.

Chapter Seven

Sunday morning Laine dressed with a sense of anticipation and dread. Drew would be here soon and she couldn't seem to keep the proper perspective about his kisses and the evening he'd spent with her and Cody.

She shouldn't be looking forward to seeing him again, to working side by side with him. That would only lead to trouble now and possibly heartache down the road.

First of all, he would soon return to Dallas. He would be there one day next week—a day trip to check on things at Casteel Consulting—and before long, he would go back for good.

Secondly, she didn't *do* brief flings. Her standards were that high, and she had Cody's emotions to consider. She wouldn't put him through inviting a man into their lives on a temporary basis. Just when he would get attached, Drew would leave.

Number three and the biggest reason of all: Drew wasn't the man for her. Charming as he could be, he was still authoritative. And everything in his manner indicated he wasn't one to let a woman get too close. Drew kept everyone at a distance—Arthur, the people he worked with, and her. If she got involved with a man, it would be with one who understood her need for emotional intimacy.

With a sigh she went into the kitchen for a piece of toast and a quick cup of coffee. Eating the toast, she watched Cody from the window. He was hard at basketball practice, as he had been every spare moment he had this weekend.

Deciding it was time she asked a few questions, she took her coffee outside. "Hi, there, Slugger," she said, sitting in the grass beside the driveway.

"Mom," he said impatiently, "you don't call someone who plays basketball 'Slugger.' That's for baseball."

"Oh."

She'd been calling him Slugger for years and this was the first time he'd objected. He was changing the status quo on her again—something that seemed to be happening every month or so, lately. She wondered if mothers of daughters went through this, too.

"So, what nickname do they use for someone who plays basketball?" she asked.

"I don't know." He studied his shot carefully and this time the ball went in. He turned to her and grinned. "How about Master of Hoops?"

Laine chuckled. "All right, Master of Hoops, what gives with the sudden frequent basketball practice?"

"Drew."

She should have guessed he would figure into the equation somehow.

"He told me how he used to get in an hour's practice every day before school. He said when he was ten, his coach wouldn't play him until the last five minutes of the game and then only if they were ahead by enough points." He backed up a few steps and tried another shot, groaning when this one didn't make it. "I can't believe Drew was ever that bad."

"He certainly isn't now."

"He said that when he was twelve, he was so much better, the coach couldn't believe he was the same kid. He played every game that year."

"And he owes his success to practice," she supplied, finally seeing the point.

"Yeah. He said it's all a matter of deciding what you want to do and how good you want to be at it, then going for it."

Drew would have that kind of determination, and he was passing some of it on to her son. Not a bad thing for a young boy. Drive and determination and a few lucky breaks along the way would earn a person his dreams.

Did Drew have any idea what a positive influence he was on Cody?

The boy's face lit up as Drew parked at the curb, then walked up the driveway toward them. When Cody tossed him the basketball, Drew dropped his gym bag, caught the ball, and easily made a basket from where he stood.

"Wow!" Cody said, awestruck. "That's how good I want to be."

Looking quite pleased, Drew carried his gym bag over to where Laine sat and placed it beside her. "Change of clothes. I demand a rematch on yesterday's water fight." He waggled his eyebrows suggestively.

Heat rushed through Laine at the memory of how the fight had started and what had followed. She couldn't allow a repeat.

"Not today," she declared. "We're painting on that side of the house and I will not have all our hard work washed away by some stray shots."

"Spoilsport," he grumbled around a laugh.

When he gazed down at her with warm humor in his eyes, Laine forgot her list of reasons against getting involved with this man. She only wanted him to hold her, to kiss her until she melted into a pool of need. She was very close to that already. Too close. And all he'd done was look at her.

"Kyle should be here in ten minutes, then we'll get started," she said, jumping to her feet. "Would you like a cup of coffee?" she asked Drew.

He shook his head. "Cody and I will do some one-on-one."

"All right!" Cody could barely contain his excitement.

She would have to talk to her son, Laine realized as she carried her mug into the kitchen. Caution him not to get too attached to Drew. Remind him that Drew's home and business were in Dallas.

Watching the pair from the kitchen window, she wondered if her warning would be too late. Cody still bore a lot of resentment toward his absent father and grandparents. Though he never talked about those feelings anymore, she knew the hurt and anger were buried in a shallow grave. Except for his mother, all his family had deserted him.

Would he view Drew's leaving as another desertion?

"Come on, come on, come on," Drew urged Cody, dribbling the basketball just out of Cody's reach. With a skill that took Laine's breath away, he would whisk the ball behind him each time it appeared Cody might take it away from him.

"You can do it, Cody," he encouraged. "Come on, think the ball into your hands."

"You're too fast for me," the boy protested.

Drew slowed his pace enough to give Cody a fighting chance. "Okay, we'll work you up to speed. Now think about this basketball and nothing else. There's nothing in this world except you and this ball. Concentrate."

I am concentrating, Laine said silently. But on the wrong thing. On him. The grace and fluidity of his movements. The width and power in his shoulders. The way the sun glinted off his rich black hair. The gentleness and encouragement in his voice as he instructed Cody.

The man was everything she wanted, needed, in her life. She could even live with his asserting his authority from time to time. The more she dealt with him, the more she was learning he could be made to see reason. But emotional intimacy, the one thing she couldn't live without, was the one thing he couldn't give her.

Laine had been unusually quiet all morning, Drew thought as they broke for lunch. Pensive. That was the word. He longed to ask what was on her mind, but he didn't have the right. And even if he did, he wasn't good at that sort of thing.

She made him want to be, though. Made him want to change a lot of things about his life, starting with a family. He thought he'd finally put that need to rest when Caro had left him. But yesterday, working and playing with Laine and her son, then spending the evening with her curled next to him on the couch... Alone in his bed he'd relived those precious moments over and over again.

He'd come to realize some part of him still needed that family he'd been searching for. He realized, too, that he was still wishing for what couldn't be. Relationships were fragile and fleeting for him. Laine made it look so easy, and perhaps for her it was. But not for him.

Now, as they ate a lunch of sandwiches and chips, he came to the realization that she deserved more from him than a brief fling. Even an affair wouldn't be enough to get her out of his system, because what he felt for her went beyond physical attraction. Her kindness, her loving spirit, her nurturing, integrity, willingness to fight to protect those she loved—everything about her captivated him.

He couldn't take advantage of her.

But he could make sure no one else did, he decided as a bearded man drove up and Cody announced, ''It's Bruce and he's brought us a new car.''

There was nothing new about the car. Fourteen years of sun and weathering had faded the paint to a lusterless yellow-green; its various dents and scrapes stood out in the glare of the noonday sun. Parked in her driveway, the midsize vehicle looked like a weary road warrior.

Drew had to wonder if this mechanic-friend was taking her for a ride, no pun intended.

''It's not much to look at on the outside,'' Bruce was telling her, ''but the engine's in great shape for as many miles as it has.''

''How many is that?'' Drew asked sharply.

"A hundred and six thousand. But the owner's had the oil changed every three months without fail, regular tune-ups, kept the fluid levels checked."

"Have you done the work yourself?" Drew pressed.

"No, but I know this couple. They're elderly and have to give up the car."

"What about the dents?" Drew continued. "How do you know the frame isn't bent, or worse?"

"I'm more concerned about engine reliability," Laine interjected.

When the mechanic popped the hood and started talking to her about valves, head gaskets and carbs, her expression went blank. Drew stepped in again. Someone had to look out for her interests.

Laine watched with a mixture of bewilderment and annoyance as Drew grilled Bruce further about the car's condition. Twice she managed to break into the exchange and tactfully insert that she trusted Bruce's judgment.

But Mr. Authority didn't take the hint. Instead he reached inside the window and started the engine. He listened, revved it a couple of times, listened, revved, then repeated the procedure.

"You'd think *he* was buying the car," Bruce said, standing beside her. Then he gave her a curious glance. "He's not, is he?"

"No," Laine snapped, reading all the implications in her friend's question. "I'm paying for it. I'll go get my checkbook."

She went into the house and came back to find Drew handing the keys to Bruce.

"She'll think about it and let you know," he told the mechanic.

"*She* can make her own decisions," Laine retorted. She turned to Bruce and snatched the car keys out of his hand. "I'll take it."

"Laine," Drew proceeded to argue, "the car has a hundred and six thousand miles on it."

She kept on writing the check. "What a coincidence. One hundred and six thousand is my lucky number." She silenced the forthcoming protest with a stern glance. "I trust Bruce's judgment," she said yet again.

Drew nodded once, then walked away to join Cody and Kyle who were cleaning up the remains of lunch. Laine sighed.

"Friend of yours?" Bruce asked.

Good question, Laine thought, a bit taken aback by the query. Just what was her relationship with Drew? They weren't lovers, but they certainly weren't just friends. They'd progressed far beyond that after the first kiss. But they couldn't be considered close friends, either. They knew next to nothing about each other.

"He's Arthur's nephew," she finally said.

"*He's* the Drew that Cody bent my ear over the other night?"

Laine nodded. "Sorry, I should have introduced you."

Bruce scratched his beard. "He didn't give you much chance to. Why don't you give me a ride back home? That way Cathy won't have to come and get me and you can test-drive the car before everything's finalized."

"Good idea."

She drove him home, then stopped at the store for milk and bread and Tootsie Rolls before heading for home herself.

"The car handled great," she commented as she got back to work on the side of the house with Drew.

"That's good," was his only reply.

She tried again as he came down the ladder. "Bruce said the tires are practically brand-new, so I won't have to buy new ones."

"Hmm."

The silent treatment—or as close to it as a person could come. She was going to scream. She watched him pick up the ladder and move it over a few feet so he could reach the next section. His knuckles were white, his jaw was set, and he clearly had nothing to say to her. She crooked a finger through one of his belt loops as he started to climb the ladder.

"What the—" His head whipped around, his dark scowl aimed at her. "What do you think you are doing?"

"Getting your attention."

"I heard every word you said. It handles great, the tires are great, everything's great."

"Except your attitude. We need to clear the air. Now."

"Fine. You wanted the car, you got it. I'm sorry I butted in."

He started up the ladder, but she jerked harder on the belt loop.

"Laine, you're going to pull me off."

"Good idea."

She planted her feet and pulled with all her might until she had him off-balance. He landed in the grass. She shoved his shoulders down, pushing him flat on his back, then planted her foot on his chest to keep him there.

He looked up at her, his gaze shocked and intrigued.

"You did not butt in," she stated emphatically.

"What else do you call it? You obviously didn't want my opinion."

"Oh," she growled. "You are so infuriating. And so stubborn!"

"I'm stubborn? If that's not a case of the pot calling the kettle—"

Splat. Her paintbrush landed in the center of his chest. Her cold, paint-filled brush. Drew felt trickles of the paint trail across his torso and down his sides.

By the time his initial shock wore off, she had turned and taken one step away. Before she could take another, he captured her delicate ankle in his firm grip. She stood perfectly still, unmoving even when he inched a little closer. Once he was close enough, he chucked her behind the knees. She landed in his arms with a startled gasp. Quickly he laid her down on the grass and straddled her slight frame.

"Don't you dare," she breathed as he lifted the dripping brush.

He was bent on retribution. He slowly brought it toward her. At the last minute she turned her head. Drew let the brush drip a pattern of drops down her neck. Squealing, she turned her head, protecting her mouth and eyes with her hands. Drew lavishly coated one arm from wrist to shoulder. He'd started on the other arm when he realized her body trembled beneath him. Fearful that he might have hurt her, he dropped the brush in the grass and gently pulled her hands from her face.

She was laughing. Uncontrollably. Her whole body shaking with the force. In a flash he felt his own fury slip away. He couldn't have held on to it if he'd tried.

But he'd expected her to be beyond livid. "What's so funny?" he asked.

"You." She pointed to his chest. "A couple of red circles and you'd have a bull's-eye."

He didn't want to grin, but he couldn't hold it back. "I figured you would be furious."

"I am. Just not at this," she explained, rubbing at the paint trickling around her neck. "I deserved this."

"And I deserved this?" he demanded, pointing to his chest.

She nodded. "You did. For making me so angry."

He shook his head. "So are you angry or not?"

"Yes." When he gave her a growl, she laughed again. "Let me up and I'll tell you."

He moved off her with a large amount of reluctance. He'd found it quite pleasant to have her beneath him. But another minute or two, and things would have gotten out of hand.

She sat on the grass, facing him. "First there's the matter of Bruce's judgment. I told you I trust him. But that doesn't mean I don't value your opinion, because I do."

"Then what was the problem?" he asked, more confused. She hadn't considered a word he'd said against the car.

"The way you handled it. You attacked him, practically put him through the third degree."

"I was just asking some questions."

Disbelief shone in her eyes.

"All right, so I might have been a bit tough. I just wanted to look out for your interests."

She sighed. "When it comes to cars, Bruce is one of those people you can count on to steer you straight, excuse the pun. The other thing that upset me is the way you automatically assumed I couldn't handle the situation on my own."

"I could see by the look on your face when he tried to tell you about the engine that you didn't understand."

"I didn't have a clue. Just like I don't know much about plumbing or wiring or fixing the microwave. But I've muddled through very successfully."

"Okay, you don't need a man."

She growled again. "That's not what I meant. I often rely on the advice and recommendations of other people, some of them men. I know you know what you're talking about. But give me credit for being able to make informed decisions. Offer advice, but don't take over."

Drew studied the ground in front of him. She was allowing him into that kinship of people she respected and valued. At the same time she was setting boundaries. He wasn't crazy about the limits, but he would have to live with that.

Did she have any idea how difficult that was going to be for him? He had a hunch she might. But did she know how much he appreciated the way she handled the situation? Except for the paintbrush-in-the-chest bit. He'd riled her to the point her temper had momentarily gotten the better of her, but she'd cooled off quickly. She'd accepted his retribution with grace and humor. Then they'd talked—no screaming or shouting, no tearful outbursts, no verbal attacks.

He looked up into her waiting gaze and knew that if he let himself, he could fall hard for her.

He cleared his throat. "In the spirit of offering advice... Laine, that car is very old."

"But it has been well taken care of. And five hundred dollars is all I can spend right now. Every penny I can spare goes into Cody's college fund."

"Oh," he said, finally understanding why she lived so frugally. "You know, I would bet he'd be able to get a full basketball scholarship. He's going to be that good a player."

"But I can't count on that. Anything could happen in the next eight years. And if he does get a scholarship, look how well-off I'll be."

He chuckled. "You'll finally be able to buy a decent car."

"Exactly." She smiled warmly at him. "You know, Cody idolizes you."

"*Idolize* is a pretty strong word."

"Hero worship. No doubt about it. The worst case I've ever seen."

Cody worshiped him. Damn, that felt good. But... "That puts a lot of responsibility on me, doesn't it?" He wouldn't let the boy down like his own father had let him down. Like Arthur had.

Laine nodded approvingly. "I knew you would realize that." Her soft sigh told him there was more on her mind. "About us..."

His breath caught. He wasn't sure he would like what she was going to say.

"I'm sure you've realized your kisses can...curl my toes, so to speak."

A grin tugged at the corners of his mouth. She was so cute and so damned sexy at the same time. "I gathered you realized it straightens out a certain part of my anatomy."

She actually blushed a little at his boldness. "Okay," she said bravely, "so we're agreed on that point. The problem is we can't take it any further."

That was the part he'd been dreading. "Because of Cody."

She nodded slowly. "If he thought we were...that there was a chance we might, you know, be serious..."

"Which we're not even considering." That's exactly what he'd been telling himself. So why did the words stick in his throat?

"Right," she agreed with an ease that cut more deeply than it should have. "I mean, you're a wonderful person, but I don't think you're the right person for me."

She was trying desperately not to hurt his feelings. Drew had to let her off the hook. "I understand." He breathed deeply and let the air out slowly. He'd never been much on baring his soul, but he had to try to let her know how he felt.

"Laine, I appreciate your honesty." He took her dainty hand in his, his thumb absently tracing a circle in the drying paint. "I've never been good at relationships. Not long-term. I wouldn't want Cody—or you—to end up hurt, once things were over."

She nodded her understanding and her unspoken agreement. This was the way it had to be, for both of them. So why did she look as if she wanted to cry, and why did he feel as though his heart was breaking?

She studied the paint on his chest and grinned. "What do you think Cody and Kyle will say when they see us?"

"Kyle will be wise enough not to say anything at all to the boss, but Cody..."

"He'll demand an explanation for sure."

It was Drew's turn to grin. "I will leave it entirely up to you to come up with one he'll buy."

"Thanks a lot."

"Come on," he said, helping her up. "We have a house to finish painting and dinner with a crotchety cardiac patient."

"Arthur?"

"Who else? He demands Emma do the cooking so you can take it easy tonight. Me, I can work myself to death."

She laughed softly. "I know he cares about you, too." She took her hand out of his. "Just friends, then?"

"Friends."

Crack. The break in his heart widened a little more.

Chapter Eight

Drew threaded his way through the Thursday-afternoon traffic out of KCI Airport south to the Plaza district, in a hurry to be back at the office again. He'd missed Laine the twenty hours he'd been in Dallas. Missed her much more than he'd expected.

He'd always loved Dallas. Knew whom to call to fill the hours, had his favorite places. But this trip, he hadn't made a single personal phone call, hadn't ventured out of his office or condo.

Because if he couldn't be with Laine, he'd preferred to be alone. He'd worked so closely with her this past week, that he'd had to leave or risk having his control snap. Just friends, he'd agreed, but all he could think about was making love to her. A day away had only made him want her more.

Some far corner of his mind warned that these feelings were way out of line, that he was heading for trouble. He'd always heeded that voice of doom before. But the memories of holding Laine, laughing with her, even sparring with her, had drowned out the fears. He needed her that badly. Needed to be with her.

Alone last night, he'd tried to figure out where his feelings for her were taking him. The conclusion was that he didn't know and he wasn't even sure he cared.

This indecisiveness was very unlike him. He believed in analyzing relationships, periodically reconsidering his course along the way, thereby leaving little to chance. Minimize the risks. That had been his motto for the biggest part of his life.

He parked in the garage and walked inside the building, wondering how one slender sprite of a woman could have him this mixed-up.

By the time the elevator opened on the fourth floor, Drew acknowledged that he probably never would understand what she was doing to him. He entered the reception area, surprised to note Mrs. Bradshaw's worried frown. She hung up the phone and rushed toward him.

"Crissie says Laine fainted," she said urgently. "In the break room."

Without waiting to hear more, Drew rushed down the hallway. Sara, Debbie and Crissie were huddled around Laine who lay stretched out on the floor. Her cheeks were bright red, but the rest of her face was as white as a sheet of computer paper. Her eyes were clouded with pain. As the other women spotted Drew, they stood to make room for him.

He knelt beside her, his heart racing in his chest. "Damn it, Laine," he said softly as he eased her head onto his lap. "If you were ill you should have made an appointment with your doctor."

She groaned. "I didn't know I was."

"All right. Can you sit up?"

She nodded, but raised a hand to her head and groaned again when she tried to move. Drew realized she was in a lot of pain. Worried, he scooped her into his arms and carried her to the couch in his office. The heat from her fevered body burned him through his suit.

"Rest here for a minute." He stroked her hair soothingly, then got up and walked over to the sink at the bar. He returned with a glass of water, two aspirin and a damp cloth, which he gently draped across her forehead once she'd swallowed the medication. "How long have you had this fever?"

She shook her head very slightly. "It's been coming on this afternoon. Along with this unbelievable headache."

Her voice was a bare whisper. Drew was thankful she had come to work today. With Cody in school for one more day, she might have been alone at the house, perhaps unable to phone for help.

"I'm calling Dr. Manning," he said, getting up to reach the phone on the desk.

She caught his hand. "No. I'm sure it's just a summer flu."

"Laine, you fainted—"

"Not really. Things just went a little fuzzy. This headache..."

He kissed her hand, then ran his fingertips over her warm skin. "This once," he said gently, "let's not argue. Please."

Laine's resistance melted at his soft plea. She was so glad to see him, so weak where he was concerned. Weak, period, at the moment. She nodded just enough to convey her acquiescence. As Drew spoke to the doctor, she listened to the genuine concern in his voice. Concern she craved from him.

She closed her eyes and quit trying to make sense of her need for his caring. For now she would just go with the flow, and be grateful he'd returned at the moment she needed his help. She didn't feel strong enough to move off this couch, let alone get herself home.

She opened her eyes at the brush of his fingers over her hot cheeks. Drew's touch. Wonderfully comforting.

"Manning said you're probably right and it's just the flu, but he said to watch you to make sure it's nothing more serious. Right now he said to get you home and into bed for the weekend."

"The weekend? This is only Thursday."

"Your weekend starts today." He gave her a sympathetic half-smile. "Did you have other plans?"

"A few, but they didn't involve an aspirin bottle and a thermometer. I need to take Cody shopping for... things he needs for... SPACE CAMP."

"Afraid that will have to wait a couple of days." He touched his finger to the tip of her nose. "If you behave yourself, maybe we could rent some movies."

He sounded just like her trying to pacify Cody when a case of the flu confined him to the house. He was being so wonderful. As if he knew that was exactly what she needed from him.

Drew helped her to his car, adjusting the seat back to a reclining position. She closed her eyes, absorbing his caring. It had been so terribly long since she'd had anyone to pamper her, to nurse her aches and pains.

And she did hurt, she thought, as Drew got her into the house and left her in her bedroom. Her head throbbed violently. Her entire body was on fire, but she was chilled to the bone. She barely managed to get out of her clothes and into a nightshirt unassisted. She sank into bed and was pulling the covers up when Cody knocked on the door and peeked in on her.

"Drew wants to know if you're decent," he said, his young brow creased with worry. Laine was rarely ill, and never had a bug knocked her out like this.

"I'll be fine tomorrow," she reassured him with a heavy sigh. *Please, heaven, let me feel better soon.* Her eyes slid closed, easing the pain in her head slightly.

"Regardless," she heard Drew say as he came into the room behind Cody, "she stays down for the weekend. She needs to get plenty of rest. She's been working too hard lately."

"Yeah, she worked really late yesterday, then helped Consuelo clean house until the ten o'clock news was over, then she had to bake cookies for the class fund-raiser we had today," Cody chimed in, his young voice holding years of protectiveness.

"An occasional long day isn't going to kill me," Laine protested weakly.

"That's not what you tell Arthur when he works too hard," Cody reminded her. He looked at Drew. "She's always telling him, and me, how important rest is."

"Well, resting is exactly what she'll be doing. She's spending the entire weekend in that bed or on the couch, nowhere else."

Laine sighed. "You don't have to talk about 'her' as if she's not in the same room with you."

The two ignored her. "And she drinks all the fruit juice we can pour down her." Drew held out a tall glass of orange juice.

"Yeah." Cody rubbed his hands together, really getting into his role as nurse. "Just like they say on TV.

Rest, drink plenty of fluids, and take . . . some kind of medicine.''

Laine would have groaned if her head had been pounding less. Drew patted Cody on the back. It was going to be a long weekend, she decided, taking the juice glass.

''Aspirin,'' Drew told Cody. ''We took care of that back at the office.''

''Then I'll go see how many cans of soup we have,'' her son informed his nursing supervisor. ''Mom hasn't been eating much this week.'' He dashed off to the kitchen.

Drew frowned down at her. ''That,'' he said, ''is one situation we will rectify immediately.''

''Please,'' she begged wearily, ''food is the last thing I want. And Cody's exaggerating.''

She handed the juice glass back to him and Drew set it on the nightstand. She'd only downed half of the juice. He wanted to push her to drink more, but noting the exhausted way she sank back onto the pillows, he didn't have the heart. He bent over her to smooth the sheet and light blanket around her shoulders.

She caught his striped tie and fingered it gently. ''You haven't worn paisley since—''

''Since you locked the one in that file cabinet,'' he supplied with a grin. ''I figured paisley unleashed the tiger in you.'' Still grinning, he pulled the tie loose from his collar and draped it over the bedpost. ''There, you can add another to your conquests.''

She laughed weakly. ''Thank you for getting me home.''

''No problem. Try to sleep.'' He brushed a strand of hair away from her face. Her skin was still hot, and apt to get hotter, he thought, walking out of the room. He left the door open a bit so he or Cody would hear her if she called.

While Cody walked Consuelo back to her side of the duplex, Drew phoned to tell his uncle he was staying with Laine and Cody and explain why.

"I knew this would happen," Arthur said, swearing like a true construction worker.

As the conversation progressed, Drew learned that Laine had been working long hours ever since Arthur's last heart attack a year ago. She'd assumed every duty that fell within her capabilities just to lighten his load. Drew gathered that the main reason Arthur had finally called him in was to provide Laine with a much-needed break.

Just what he wanted to hear, Drew thought. But his irritation soon faded as he tried to coax her to take a few spoonfuls of the soup he and Cody had heated. She drank some of the broth, but ate little of the chicken or vegetables.

"She didn't eat, did she?" Cody asked as Drew carried the bowl back to the kitchen.

"We'll try again later. What are you doing?" he asked, noticing the boy was busy jotting something on a piece of paper.

"Making a list of Mom's favorite foods. She always buys my favorites when I'm sick. I thought Dennis could take me to the store so you could stay with Mom in case she needs something."

"Good thinking," Drew said. The boy was doing everything he could to take care of his mom. Protectiveness mixed with a caring that ran deep. Bonds unlike anything Drew had ever experienced.

"I don't know what to do about money, though," Cody continued. "Mom always writes a check."

This was one area Drew could handle. He passed the boy a handful of bills. "Stock up."

"Okay. Then Mom won't have to go to the store when she feels better. What about dinner for us?"

Drew hadn't thought that far ahead yet. His only concern was what he could coax Laine to eat. He wasn't much of a cook. "Pizza?" he asked the boy.

"Works for me." Cody got up and reached for the phone. "I'll order the pizza first, then I'll call Dennis and tell him to pick me up in about an hour."

Drew nodded once, then left to go check on Laine. She was lying on her side, her back to the door. He called softly to her. When she didn't answer, he walked around to the other side of the bed. Her eyes were closed, her breathing even, her brow smoother.

He watched her sleep for a long moment, feeling a peacefulness fill him. Here the restlessness was gone. Here there was nothing to prove, nothing to do except simply be. Gazing down at her sleeping form, he realized how emotionally weary he truly was.

What was this woman doing to his well-ordered life?

He adjusted the blanket over her shoulder, then left. Cody was in the living room, playing a video game.

"Mom okay?" the kid asked.

"She's sleeping."

For lack of anything else to do, Drew sat beside Cody and watched him try to land his aircraft on the carrier while dodging bursts of antiaircraft fire. By the time Cody had used up all his tries, Drew was hooked. Cody showed him how to work the control pad and coached him through the game. Before they knew it, the pizza had arrived.

Cody put the box on the coffee table, opened it and inhaled the delicious aroma, then went to the kitchen, returning with three plates. Drew went to peek in on Laine.

Seeing her eyes were open, he frowned. "The door-bell woke you."

"I was half-awake before it rang." She sniffed the air. "Must have been pizza delivery."

He had to chuckle. "At least your nose is fine. Are you hungry?"

She shook her head. "Maybe later." Her eyes drifted closed.

He would definitely work on her appetite when she felt better, Drew vowed silently. For now, he would let her be. She was obviously miserable. He left her to sleep, checking on her every half hour or so. Each time, she was still awake and feeling worse than the time before.

A little after eight o'clock, Cody and Dennis re-turned from the grocery store.

"We got her two favorite kinds of ice cream, the juice bars and Popsicles she likes best, cookies, apples—"

"And these." Dennis dug out a bag of Tootsie Roll miniatures and dropped it on the table.

"Tootsie Rolls?" Drew asked.

"They're for times of stress, she says," Dennis ex-plained. "She stashes them everywhere."

"Why?"

"So they're not so easy to find," Cody told him. "If she has to hunt for them and try to remember where she put them, she doesn't eat so many of them."

Drew guessed there was a certain logic in that. He opened the box of juice bars and took one in to Laine. "Try this," he said, holding the frozen strawberry bar out to her.

"They're too cold to eat and my head hurts too hard," she said around a moan.

"Maybe we should call Dr. Manning," Cody suggested, having followed Drew into Laine's room.

"I'm fine," Laine roused herself enough to tell her son firmly. "You don't need to disturb Dr. Manning when there's nothing he can do for me. I'll just have to wait this flu out."

Realizing the boy was genuinely worried about his mother, Drew put his arm around Cody's shoulders. "If she's not better by morning, we'll call him then," he promised. "Meanwhile let's get the groceries put away."

"Groceries?" Laine asked. "How many and who paid for them?"

"When you're feeling up to it," Drew stated, "we'll talk about it."

"Yeah," Cody chimed in. "Right now you should be sleeping."

But sleep seemed to elude her. At ten o'clock Drew sent Cody to bed and went in to check on Laine again. One look at the misery in her eyes and he decided he couldn't leave her. He sat on the edge of the bed.

"What can I do for you?" he asked softly.

Laine sighed and shook her head, knowing only time would make her feel better. She was hot and chilled at the same time. Her mouth was dry despite all the fluids he and Cody had insisted she drink. And despite the aspirin they insisted she take, her joints still ached and her head throbbed. She couldn't get comfortable.

But through it all, Drew had been here. Was still here. Worry creased his features each time he leaned over her bed. She didn't have the strength to make sense of his concern, or of her own willing dependence on him.

Later she would sort out the reasons, but for now she needed to cling to someone. To him.

"How about my trading places with you?" he offered.

She smiled weakly. "You don't know what you're asking."

"I have a pretty good idea." He brushed his hand over her forehead. "Still warm. How about some more juice?"

She nodded. He held the glass while she took several sips, then set it back on the nightstand.

"Think you could sleep?" he asked.

She'd passed the point of exhaustion years ago, it seemed, but she hadn't been able to rest. Neither had he, she thought, studying the weariness in his eyes.

From where her head lay on the pillow, she saw the striped necktie hanging on the bedpost. The silk reminded her of how he'd been there when she needed him, how he was still there for her though he should be home in his own bed.

"I should send you home," she murmured. She didn't want him to leave, but it must be late.

His expression clouded. "Do you want me to go?"

She should lie. Some panicky inner voice warned that they'd passed a milestone in their association. To continue on the same course would create complications that would have to be dealt with. But her need for the comfort she gained from his ministrations won out.

She laid her hand along the side of his unshaven jaw. "Stay?" she asked hesitantly.

He kissed her palm, then stroked his thumb over her skin. Delicious ripples of anticipation flowed through her.

She was sick, feverish and yet his touch could still make her senses come alive. How could she react so strongly to him?

She shouldn't cling to him, shouldn't lean on him, but she desperately needed to be nurtured, to experience more of his caring. Too soon it would be gone. She closed her eyes against the hot tears that threatened.

Drew kicked off his shoes and stretched out on the bed beside her. He would have been devastated, had she sent him home. It felt so good to have her need him.

"Drew," she whispered, blinking her eyes open, "what's your college like?"

"Texas A & M?" Surprised by the unexpected question, he glanced sharply at her. "Why?"

"Cody has decided that's where he wants to go."

"Really?"

Cody wanted to go to the college he'd attended, Drew thought with a feeling of warmth. The satisfying glow stayed with him as he told her about some of his fraternity pranks. She smiled at the outrageous tales, even chuckled a few times. Drew realized she didn't have the strength to do more. He talked on, telling her about some of his favorite classes and professors, hoping she would drift off to sleep. But when he ran out of stories, she was still awake.

"How about the basketball?" she asked. "Did you enjoy that?"

"I did when I was winning games and being voted MVP."

"You don't do many things just for the fun of it, do you?"

He sighed. "I think I've forgotten how, if I ever knew. Coming out on top has been the most important thing in my life for a long time."

''What about Arthur?''

''He's important, too.''

She angled her head to peer up at him. ''Would you do one thing for me, as a friend? Would you tell Arthur he's important to you?''

''I dropped everything to be here when he called me. That should say it all.''

''Just promise me you'll say the words to him. Soon. Please.'' She laid a hand on his arm, as if to emphasize that this was something he had to do.

''I promise,'' he agreed, studying her hand on his arm. He didn't for a minute think talking to his uncle would change anything between them, but if it was this important to her, he would give it his best shot.

He laid his hand over hers, noting her skin was still too warm.

''What time is it?'' she asked as he reached for the glass of juice on the nightstand.

''Midnight. More juice?''

When she nodded, he gave her a drink, then got a cool cloth to lay across her forehead. She sighed gratefully, but he could see she was no closer to sleep than before.

''Laine,'' he said softly. ''Should I have Cody call your parents in the morning? Let them know—''

''They haven't had anything to do with me since my divorce,'' she said tightly.

''But they're your parents. Cody's grandparents.''

''They are very traditional people. Very rigid. They were appalled when I divorced Cody's father. They said if I left Ernie, that would be the last straw.''

''Last straw?''

She nodded. ''I'd rebelled against their restrictions most of my life. I wanted to play volleyball, but they insisted piano lessons were more suited to a young lady. They were livid when they discovered I'd found a way to work in volleyball practice between school and piano lessons. Then I insisted on getting a job and going to community college at night.''

"How could they object to that?"

"A young lady was supposed to get married. Taking care of her husband and having children was supposed to be her life's work."

"But that's antiquated nonsense."

"Mom and Dad stayed stuck in their own time warp, out of sync with the rest of the world. I was in such a hurry to escape from home that I married at nineteen and was pregnant before I realized Ernie's idea of a relationship was as antiquated as my parents'. When I finally got up the courage to file for a divorce, they all made it clear Cody and I were on our own."

"They've stuck to that all these years?" he asked, feeling irrationally angry at the thought of Laine's parents practically abandoning the boy and turning their backs on her.

"I still send letters occasionally, Christmas cards, pictures of Cody. I've never gotten an answer. Now my life, and Cody's, is here."

"With Arthur," he said quietly.

"Arthur's the father I always wanted. He offered to take care of Cody if anything happened to me, and I accepted gladly. I couldn't send him to my parents, even if they would take him. It would be like sentencing him to prison."

Drew thought of the boy's spirit, his generosity and caring, and knew Laine was right.

"So about three years ago I asked Arthur to be Cody's guardian if anything should happen to me."

She'd been that close to his uncle, but Arthur had never mentioned her until a week ago in his office. That hurt.

"Arthur's health is so uncertain," he reminded her.

"I know, but there isn't anyone else I could trust to look after Cody. Except you," she finished around a small yawn.

Drew's breath caught. She would trust him with the most important thing in her life—her son. He would never be able to put into words how much that meant to him.

"Hopefully Cody will never have to do without his mother," Drew said sincerely.

To his surprise, he found himself telling her how his mother had died in a boating accident at the Lake of the Ozarks. He'd never been close to his father, and after his mother's death, the distance between them had widened into a chasm he hadn't been able to bridge before his father's death. Arthur, too, had become more distant than before. His invitations for Drew to stay in Kansas City had become less frequent.

Drew found the words poured out easily, as if he'd waited all these years to confide in someone, in Laine. He'd never made friends easily. He was always afraid of trying and failing, afraid he would get a glimpse of real caring, only to have the door slammed in his face. Yet he craved the intimacy his friends had with their families. Craved the intimacy Laine had with his uncle.

As he talked, Laine heard the loneliness and hurt in his voice. Her heart swelled with sympathy for the boy who'd never had someone to hold him when he cried. But while their childhoods had been similar, they'd grown into two very dissimilar people.

She sought the companionship of other people, the warmth and friendships she'd missed while growing up. Drew still lived his pain. He protected his heart from further hurt with suspicions and mistrust—a very lonely way to live.

"Do you remember much about your mother?" she asked.

"Mostly that she liked to laugh, and that my father was less somber when she was around."

"Tell me more about her," she persisted when he grew quiet.

"I remember how my father looked at her whenever she walked into a room. Like he was seeing her for the first time, and each time he was totally bewitched all over again."

"That's the way love should be," she mumbled groggily. "Not one person trying to own or dominate the other. Was she pretty?"

"Yes. But thinking back to the things I remember about her, I believe what caught your attention was her personality, her liveliness, her caring...."

Laine closed her eyes, feeling sleep overtake her. She didn't want to give in to its demand yet, not with Drew letting down some of his defenses, not when she was finally gaining some insight into him. There was real communication in this middle-of-the-night conversation, an honest sharing of feelings without pride or defensiveness getting in the way. She feared she might never find this with him again. He didn't open himself to others easily. This gift was rare, one to be treasured.

His mother's death had left a big hole in his life, Drew mused, listening to Laine's even breathing. Caro had enlarged that hole to a bottomless chasm. Her vibrancy, so similar to his mother's, had attracted him the

moment he met her. He'd once thought she possessed
his mother's caring, but it had been a well-rehearsed
act. He'd wanted so badly for it to be genuine that he
ignored the signs telling him otherwise. He'd set himself up for that fall.

He gazed at Laine's lovely face, relieved to note she
was sleeping at last. Was she genuine? Could he take a
chance and trust once more?

Chapter Nine

As Laine listened, the birds in the tree outside her window cheerily welcomed the dawn. Her joints still ached with fever, but at least her head had eased its unbearable pounding while she slept. She should get up, but she was much too comfortable to move. She burrowed deeper into the bed's inviting warmth, then gradually realized it was Drew's warmth and his body she was cozying up to.

She slowly opened her eyes and turned her head to look up at him. His hair was tousled and a dark stubble covered his chiseled jaw. Again the attraction she felt every time she saw him swamped her. With it came the realization that he'd stayed to care for her, had given her what comfort he could.

No man had ever shown her such tenderness, she thought with a sigh. Could this really be the same man who had once treated her with cold disdain? The man Arthur had said was as cold as an iceberg?

Studying Drew's sleep-softened features, she wondered if Arthur had a clue how warm and giving his nephew could be, if the older man had any idea just how deep Drew's caring nature went. Perhaps Drew himself didn't know.

Perhaps they all would get a chance to find out, she thought, turning to see the clock on the nightstand behind her. A quarter to six. The alarm was set to go off in another fifteen minutes. She gave a very brief thought to going in to work before deciding she wouldn't make it as far as the shower. She reached to shut off the alarm, then lay back down.

Drew rolled toward her and dropped a heavy arm across her middle. "You're not going anywhere today," he growled sleepily in her ear.

"Lucky for you I don't have the strength to argue the point," she said, savoring the warmth of him so close to her side.

His breath fanning her hair sent tremors of excitement racing through her body. It would be so wonderful to be able to wake up next to him every morning. To give herself up to the thrill of being in his arms. He began to nuzzle her ear and she knew her control was tenuous at best.

"Drew," she said quietly.

"Hmm," came his groggy reply. His hand caressed its way up her arm to her shoulder.

Laine felt her weak resistance fade a little more. "Drew," she said insistently.

He stopped in midbreath and sat up. "I . . . I'm sorry. . . . I guess I was getting carried away," he finished.

A major understatement if ever there was one. He'd begun to think how perfectly her curves fit against the length of him, and that thought had brought on the longing to explore each and every one of those curves.

He shouldn't have fallen asleep here in her bed, but he'd been exhausted. Once she'd fallen asleep, he found the thought of leaving her too much to bear. He had craved her warmth, that afterglow of the closeness they'd shared. He hadn't wanted to be alone, and when she'd unconsciously cuddled up to him, he'd decided he wasn't going anywhere.

Amazing as it was, his feelings hadn't changed with the dawn. But still, he was afraid she would want more from him than he could give.

Yawning, he eased over to his side of the bed. "What time does Cody get up for school?" he asked, already missing her being close.

"Six-thirty. But he'll get himself up."

Still, Drew didn't think it would be a good idea to have the boy find him in Laine's bed. The situation might be innocent enough, but he was wishing things were altogether different. He wasn't sure how Cody would react to this situation.

"I . . . I'll put on some coffee," he said. "Would you like some?"

"It'll be a welcome change from juice and water."

Stretching his stiff back muscles, Drew went into the kitchen. He had started a pot of coffee and was contemplating whether he could coax Laine into eating something when Cody came downstairs.

"Did you stay all night?" he asked, taking in Drew's rumpled appearance.

Drew nodded. "Your mom didn't fall asleep until after two o'clock."

"Is she still asleep?"

Drew shook his head. "I think the birds woke her."

Cody gave a heavy sigh. "It's that birdbath and those feeders she's got. Every bird in the city must come here."

She was a true nurturer, Drew thought, opening a cabinet and gazing at the boxes of cereal. Bran flakes with and without raisins. Corn flakes. Instant oatmeal. And one box of cookie-flavored bits.

"That's for snacks," Cody said. "She takes the box on the back porch and shares with Bones, this big old dog who used to dig up her garden. She taught him to come to the back door and bark for her to come out and feed him treats. He quit digging."

Anyone else would have called Animal Control and had the dog picked up. "So you think you could get her to eat something?"

While Cody went to hopefully entice Laine into eating, Drew rummaged though the cabinet for coffee mugs, sugar and creamer. At the office, he'd noticed that she put generous amounts of both in her coffee. He filled the mugs, then carried one in to her.

Cody perched on the edge of her bed. "And just watch, Mr. Kissinger will try to give us homework."

"It's your last day," Laine said quietly.

"That won't stop Mr. K." He turned to Drew. "She didn't want anything yet. Are you going to stay with her?"

"That's not necessary," Laine protested when Drew nodded.

"Sure, it is," Cody stated. "I have to go all day today to make up for a snow day, and you shouldn't leave someone sick alone to fend for himself. That's what you always say. And Consuelo can't stay with you. Even a little cold really knocks her out." He leaned over and laid a hand across her forehead. "See, you're still hot. How's the headache?"

"Almost bearable," she said, hiding a small smile at his nursing.

"Okay." He stood and gave her a quick kiss on the forehead. "I'll come say goodbye before I leave for school," he said solemnly.

Drew saw the look of pride and concern flit across Laine's face as she watched Cody walk out of the room. Drew handed her the mug. "You and Cody really look after each other."

"I worry that he's had to grow up too fast. I do depend on him a lot."

"There's plenty of kid left in him along with the boy-growing-up. Speaking of which, I've had the hand weights in the trunk of my car all week. What did you decide?"

"That my life was much easier when he was four and the worst of my problems was his bugging me for an ice-cream cone before dinner."

"Has it been hard for you, raising Cody alone?" he asked with a tenderness Laine knew she could become dependent upon.

"At times. Not the having-him part. He's added so much to my life. It's the parenting part. Having no one else to confide in, no one else to share the responsibilities." She sighed. "I wouldn't trade my son for anything, but sometimes I do feel overwhelmed."

She sipped her coffee, enjoying this moment with Drew, being able to talk to him this way. She'd hoped the closeness they'd shared last night would linger on into the morning.

"You have to let him grow up," Drew said quietly.

"I know. I can't hold him down, and I don't want to. It's just that each age brings its own set of complications. I'd just gotten a handle on the current ones."

"You're doing a wonderful job with him," he offered, studying her with a warmth in his gaze that went deeper than the sexual hunger she'd seen before.

"Thanks." Something was happening between them—something that held the promise of everything she'd ever wanted. "You noticed how I drink my coffee," she said.

"A touch of coffee and lots of cream and sugar." He smiled. The thump of Cody's feet on the stairs echoed through the room. "He does everything with such spirit."

"That's why I'm afraid he'll go overboard on this weights thing."

"I'll talk to him, if you'd like."

Did he know how much his asking her permission meant to her? How much she treasured the consideration he was showing her?

"Cody would probably take instruction from you better than another lecture from Mom," she told him with a wry smile.

"Then you've got it. I'll give him the weights after school and I'll stress the importance of keeping the proper perspective. Do you want to be the one to tell him about the weights?"

She finished the rest of her coffee, then shook her head. "I get the feeling this is strictly a guy thing with him. Personal and sort of private."

"Does that bother you?"

"Some. But I understand, so I'll stay out of it, give him a little room to himself." She handed Drew her empty coffee cup. "Thank you."

With a nod, Drew took her mug, then carried it into the kitchen. She was such a trusting, giving person, and she trusted him to do right by her son. He wondered if she had any idea how much that meant to him. He would do his utmost not to let her down.

As he placed the mug in the sink, Cody set a jar of peach preserves on the countertop next to a loaf of bread.

"That's Mom's favorite jelly," he said, pushing the toaster toward Drew.

"Okay. Toast and jelly. I'll make sure she eats some."

"Then takes a nap," Cody emphasized.

Drew nodded. "By the way, she gave the go-ahead to the—"

"Weights? All right! I knew you could make her see things our way."

Our way, Drew mused, liking the sound of it. "They're in the trunk of my car," he told the boy. "When you come home from school, I'll—"

"Teach me the best exercises?"

Laine hadn't exaggerated the boy's enthusiasm. "Right, and a couple of other things." Such as keeping things in perspective, as he'd promised Laine. And perhaps a few of the finer points in the power of persuasion.

The honk of a horn outside brought Cody's head up from the bowl of cereal he'd just poured and begun devouring. "Gotta go. Thanks."

He ran out, tore past the sofa and TV, poked his head into his mom's room to say goodbye, then raced to the door, grabbing his key from the table in front of the picture window.

If Drew hadn't seen it with his own eyes, he wouldn't have believed anyone could disappear so fast. He would have to help Cody find a way to get that kind of speed and focus into his basketball.

That was when it hit him. Without realizing it, he'd begun to think of his relationship with mother and son as an ongoing thing.

He liked Cody and felt a rare kinship with the kid. The way Cody hung on his every word... Drew had the respect of a lot of people—businesspeople. As that reporter for the *Wall Street Journal* had said, he had some very creative, yet legal, ways of salvaging a company.

With Cody, though, there was more than admiration for Drew's basketball prowess. They'd established a friendship. Whatever the future held, he hoped that would never change.

As he dropped two slices of whole-wheat bread into the toaster, he thought about Laine and how she approved of his involvement in her son's life. She could resent the fact that Cody was turning to someone else for advice. Instead she encouraged the boy to reach out to others—to Drew.

Then there was the way she'd leaned on him when he'd found her ill. This independent, assertive woman had allowed him to carry her to the couch in his office, allowed him to care for her—something he hadn't known he could do. She'd also talked to him about her hurt at her parents' rejection and her worries and fears for her son.

It was wonderful to feel needed, satisfying to have Laine cling to him. He wanted that to last a long time, but knew how unlikely that was. Everything he knew about relationships could be summed up in three words: *they never lasted.* Then why was the need to protect and comfort this particular woman so strong?

Since his mother's death, he'd practiced the art of detachment. But Laine had somehow gotten through the barriers, and he sensed there was nothing he could do to rebuild the breaks.

The thought of making love to her no longer startled or surprised him. He'd been wanting her for days. Hell, he couldn't stop thinking about her—erotic images, tender feelings, a desire to shelter her from any problem she had to face. He didn't believe in "forever" for himself, but she made him want to.

This woman was changing his life. Regardless of what he wanted or how much he resisted, it was happening. He wished he could give in to the needs and longings he felt, but the risks were so great.

Lying on her bed, Laine opened her eyes when she heard the back door in the kitchen open. She glanced at the clock. Two forty-five. Too early for Cody to be home, so it must be Drew.

She smiled to herself, thinking of how she'd told him to stay at the office as long as he was needed, that she intended to sleep. Regardless, he'd told her, he'd promised Cody he would stay with her, and he was determined to be away for no more than two hours. He was ten minutes early.

He rapped lightly on the bedroom door. If she hadn't been awake, she would never have heard it.

"Come in," she said.

He pushed open the door and walked in, looking devastating as always in his dark suit. "Did you sleep?"

She nodded. "I just woke up a few minutes ago. My stomach started growling."

His brow arched in pleased surprise. "When Dennis delivered the changes of clothes I wanted, he brought some of Emma's chicken and noodles."

"Really? You wouldn't tease a starving woman, would you?"

He chuckled. "Emma said if anything could resurrect your pitiful appetite, this would be it. I'll go heat some up."

When he left the room, Laine went to the bathroom to freshen up. Her short hair was tousled, but not in too bad shape for all the tossing and turning she'd done the last twenty-some hours. She combed it, brushed her teeth, ran some cool water over her face, then decided that would have to do.

Drew was taking a bowl out of the microwave when she walked into the kitchen. He frowned at her.

"I couldn't wait for you to bring it to me," she said, sitting down at the table. "And I had to get out of that room."

His glower changed to a grin as she dipped her spoon into the bowl he placed in front of her. As she ate, he slipped off his suit coat and tie and hung them on the pegs by the back door. She noticed a small duffel on the floor beside his briefcase.

From the look of things, he planned on being around quite a bit this weekend, and she decided she was delighted with the prospect. Gazing across the table at him, studying his well-defined features—his rich black hair and his strikingly deep blue eyes—she knew she would miss him very much when he left.

"How were things in Dallas?" she asked as he heated a second helping of the chicken and noodles for her once she'd finished the first.

"I'm out of the office so often, as a rule, that I've got everything to where it runs smoothly all the time."

" 'Out of the office' as in traveling?"

He placed the second helping in front of her, then glanced at his watch. "I should be on my way to Atlanta right about now."

"Atlanta?" It was her fault he was still here in K.C., tending to her needs instead of his company's. "Drew, you should have gone. I could have—"

"What? Collapsed in the break room again? Once of that is enough."

"But—"

He laughed. "Laine, this is where I wanted to be. I could have explained to Cody that I had to leave, and had Emma come stay with you this afternoon."

"He really would have understood."

"I realize that. But I've been sending Jake Tanner on smaller assignments for two years now. It's time he tackled bigger and better things. Besides, it's the boss's privilege to pull the plum assignments."

So she was a plum assignment. His tone had been lighthearted, but there was a seriousness in the depths of his eyes that told her those middle-of-the-night moments had meant something to him. While holding her hand and plying her with aspirin and juice wasn't how he'd planned to spend his time, she'd needed him and he'd rearranged things so he could take care of her.

"I did make one concession to work, though," he commented as she finished the second bowlful. "I rented a fax machine. The store should deliver it this afternoon. I may tie up the phone line."

"That's no problem for me, and Cody will gladly miss a call or two if it's for you." She stretched and stood. "I think I'll camp out in front of the TV for a while. I need a change of scenery."

He got her pillow and blanket and helped her get situated, then went to clean up the small mess he'd made in the kitchen. Laine closed her eyes, savoring the rightness of the situation and wishing it could last.

She awoke about three hours later as Cody and Drew came in the back door. Cody tiptoed into the living room.

Seeing her eyes were open, he called out to Drew, "She's awake so we can eat now." He dropped two rented movies on the floor in front of the TV, then felt her forehead. "You're still a tiny bit warm."

"But feeling better, Dr. Sullivan."

"We got Chinese for dinner," he told her as he headed back to the kitchen to help Drew dish it up.

As they ate around the coffee table, Cody chattered on about the game of one-on-one he and Drew had played after school, then about the exercises and instruction Drew had given him, then about their trip to rent the movies.

"We got an Indiana Jones—the very first one because Drew hasn't seen any of his movies. Can you believe that?" Cody asked incredulously.

Drew shrugged. "None of my dates were interested."

There it was again, that mention of the other women in his life. She had no right to let it get to her, but it did just the same.

"You're in for a real treat," Laine told him. "Action, adventure, excitement, and all the gore to go with it."

"I figured as much, from what Cody described," he said. "We got you a romantic comedy."

The man was turning out to be the epitome of thoughtfulness, she decided as she finished the last bite of her egg roll. She lay back down on the couch, basking in the glow of happiness she felt.

"Can we watch the Indiana Jones first?" Cody begged her. "You know the parts where you have to shut your eyes."

"We rented movies because your mom's not feeling well," Drew reminded him. "We should give her first choice."

"That's okay," she said. "I do like Harrison Ford."

Stretched out on the couch during the movie, Laine noted the close rapport Drew and Cody had established. That Cody was very taken with Drew was more evident the longer she observed the pair. They fussed over her as the movie progressed, Cody parroting his mentor. Did she need a blanket? A drink? A frozen-juice bar? When one wasn't asking, the other was. And both were thoroughly relishing the parts of the flick that made Laine squeamish.

Cody needed a male role-model in his life. He idolized Drew. But how long would Drew be a part of their lives? When his work at Masters Construction was completed, he would go back to Texas. After he'd inherited the company, Drew would probably hire someone else to run it so he could devote his time to his own business. When that happened, he would have no reason to return to Kansas City.

She had no idea how to prepare Cody for the inevitable separation, or how to prepare herself. Last weekend painting the house and these past two days with him taking care of her, she'd come to enjoy having Drew nearby. His strength, his tenderness, the rare sharing of his feelings, had been too much to resist. During the night, both of them had talked about things they'd kept to themselves until now. She'd never felt so close to another human being.

Her last thought before dozing off in the middle of the movie was that she would be very lonely without him. She woke up when someone lightly shook her and opened her eyes to see Drew looking down at her.

"Time to hit the sack for real," he said.

"I missed the movie ending," she said around a yawn.

"You've seen it before, but if you want to see it again, you'll have to watch it tomorrow. You need your sleep."

"Drew's right," her son said, dropping a kiss on her cheek. "He thinks you'll be all right by yourself tonight. Will you?"

"I'm fine now, sweetheart," she told him.

He nodded, then went upstairs to get ready for bed himself.

"He's something else," Drew said, helping her up and walking her to her room.

"He is. But first Arthur and now you are turning him into another overprotective male. He listens to the two of you fuss over me, then carries it to extremes sometimes."

"He's concerned about you because he cares," Drew explained.

Was that the reason behind Drew's own concern? she longed to ask. "So you're telling me that the smothering goes with the caring?" she asked with a soft laugh.

"Precisely."

He left to get her another two aspirin and put a fresh glass of juice on the nightstand in case she got thirsty during the wee hours, then tucked her under the covers. There was a hunger in his eyes when he said good-night—a hunger she longed to unleash, then satisfy completely.

After he'd locked up the house and left, Laine realized his striped tie still hung over the bedpost, a tangible reminder of her roller-coaster relationship with him.

On their first day together, her fury over his attempts to dominate and her shock at the power of his kiss had driven her to lock the end of his paisley tie in that file-cabinet drawer. Now there was the striped tie he'd worn yesterday, a symbol of his caring.

Life certainly hadn't been dull since he'd arrived on the scene. He was infuriating and challenging, caring and sexy, and tempting beyond reason. There was a thrill in matching wits with him. She wondered if she could ever live with him, but the thought of life without him left her feeling empty.

Still, she knew that long after the lust had abated, she would have to deal with the man's other traits... his forceful personality, his need to run everything himself. And there was the emotional intimacy she longed for. Was what they'd shared last night a fluke, or the start of something more?

Chapter Ten

Drew was going to explode with seven kinds of frustration—mainly exasperation at Laine's stubbornness. In this twenty-minute argument, she had held her ground solidly. What a way to spend a Sunday evening.

"Damn it, Laine, you need time to recuperate."

"Don't swear at me, and I've already agreed that I need a short vacation and that this is the perfect time to take it, with you here to run the office."

"Then what's the problem?" he fairly shouted.

"You are telling and not asking."

'If we want the same thing, why does it matter?"

"It just does."

He growled, clenching his fists at his sides to keep from strangling her. "I can't believe you." He looked to Cody. "Is she always this unreasonable?"

The kid shrugged. "Arthur says he trained her too

well. She used to be timid, but now when someone pushes, she pushes back—harder.''

''I can't imagine she was ever timid,'' Drew stated, glaring at her. ''Did she ever tell you how she managed to sneak in volleyball practice and games between school and piano lessons?''

''No. Tell me about it.''

Laine gave her son a narrowed stare. ''Cody, weren't you going to Buzzie's?''

The boy grabbed the basketball video game Drew had bought him, kissed his mother's cheek, then walked up to Drew. ''Trust me,'' he said, leaning close. ''I sympathize with you, but I know Mom. Arthur says that with her you have to plan your strategy, and finesse is the key. He says most women are that way.''

Laine's mouth dropped open. ''Why, that old coot. I'm going to have to watch what he's teaching you.''

''He told me I shouldn't say anything about this in front of you, but it seemed like Drew could use a little advice.''

''Thanks, pal,'' Drew said with a pleased smile.

''Sure. No problem.'' He patted Drew on the back. ''Buzzie's number is on the board by the phone. Call me when dinner's ready.''

He walked out the door, leaving Laine and Drew staring at each other for a long moment. Finally Laine laughed.

''Just who was the most adult one here?'' she queried with a wide grin.

Drew ran his hand across the back of his neck, releasing the tightness there, then slowly grinned. ''Neither of us, obviously.''

He draped his arm heavily around her shoulders, trying hard to resist the urge to attempt kissing her into submission on this issue. It might not change her mind, but it would be fun trying.

She didn't seem to realize how close he was to snapping, to taking her in his arms and kissing her until she melted. He wanted her so damned much.

Wanting had never been so complicated until now. Always before, if he wanted and the woman wanted, they went to bed. But with Laine he couldn't take the matter so lightly. He couldn't complicate their relationship any more than it already was, couldn't have her regret what passed between them in any way. He would never be able to stand it if her caring were to turn to contempt.

"So what do you say to a vacation?" he asked.

Her arm hooked around his waist, fitting there so perfectly she could have been made just for him.

"Tell me about it while you check the charcoal," she said. "I'm starving."

To Drew's delight, her appetite had returned surprisingly strong. As they walked by the pantry in the kitchen, he reached in and grabbed a handful of Tootsie Roll miniatures, passing several to her. Outside he settled her in the wooden swing in the backyard and sat beside her.

"Aren't you going to check the grill?" Laine asked, popping a piece of the candy into her mouth. "Arthur should be here in another fifteen minutes or so."

"Dinner will have to wait until . . ."

She groaned. "Until I say I will take next week off. Drew, you're being your usual pushy self." And he was much too close. His face was only a warm breath away. His cologne, the smell of him—she wanted to bury her nose in his neck and inhale his scent. He was turning her inside out with wanting. Couldn't he see that?

"Then we'll have to try this."

Drew leaned over and did what he'd wanted to do since he got back from Dallas. Even before that. He kissed her.

She tasted of passion and chocolate. A sweetness beyond belief. All the while, he tried to ignore the way her breasts rose and fell with her breath, tried to fight down the desire to slide his hand under her T-shirt and caress her creamy skin.

Her lips were kitten soft. He was sinking, drowning, going down and still coming back for more. He ran his hands through her silken hair. Each strand wrapped around his fingers, capturing him, tying him to her—a noose, a lifeline. When her tongue met his, the tidal wave of longing carried him further out to sea, casting him adrift in uncharted waters.

Laine was lost in the sensations he awakened. She wound her fingers in his thick hair and pulled him closer. She drank of his tender and fiery passion and was drawn into a maelstrom of heat, joy, longing, trepidation. He kissed her collarbone, her throat, the column of her neck, and nuzzled her jaw. Delicious shivers coursed through her at the light scrape of his evening beard against her skin.

She moaned softly at the tantalizing feel of his teeth gingerly nipping her earlobe. His breath bathed the side of her face with warmth. Then his mouth returned to hers in a reunion full of intensity and desire, fireworks and repressed longings, starlight and lightning.

This was new to her, this whirlwind of feelings and passions so strong it sucked her into undreamed-of depths. All she could do was cling to him. Nothing had ever felt so right.

He could continue kissing her forever, Drew thought, drugged with the taste of her. He was just beginning to realize how special this woman was.

She was soft, generous, and so unbelievably passionate. She made him feel invincible. Somehow, before he'd realized what was happening, she'd insinuated herself into his emotions. The day of reckoning would arrive eventually, and he had no idea how he would deal with the fallout.

But he refused to dwell on that now. "If you take some time off," he said, nibbling her ear again, "so will I. We can . . ."

This was all moving too fast, Laine thought with a jolt. "Drew, we agreed—"

"Angel, the friendship-only thing never stood a chance," he insisted, his eyes still dark and full of hunger. "We both knew that from the start."

"But we . . . I . . . can't," she finished on a groan as he began nuzzling her neck, scattering her objections on the evening breeze.

She tried in vain to steel her resolve, but when he did such crazy things to her senses, she couldn't think straight. She had reasons for not getting involved with him, but she couldn't recall a one.

"Then what do we do now?" she asked on a sigh.

"Check the grill," he said, abruptly raising his head from her neck.

Only then did Laine realize Arthur was watching them from the doorway at the back of the garage. Dennis stood behind him. Lost in Drew's kisses, she hadn't heard the Lincoln pull up, hadn't heard Dennis getting Arthur and the wheelchair out. As Dennis wheeled the older man over the threshold, Arthur glowered at Drew.

"What's going on?" Arthur demanded.

"I'm trying to convince Laine to take that vacation," Drew said tightly.

Laine realized his irritation was directed at his uncle. He obviously didn't appreciate Arthur's annoyance with him over what had just transpired.

"I thought you arranged the vacation Friday," Arthur said.

"With everyone but me, apparently," Laine said sharply. "I'm just now hearing about it."

"When Drew told me you had the flu, he asked me when you last had some time off. And when I got to figuring it out, it's been more than two years," Arthur said guardedly. "One thing led to another and we decided you should take a vacation."

"You decided," Laine muttered, then turned to Dennis. "Would you mind helping Drew in the kitchen? The potatoes and ears of corn are in the refrigerator and the aluminum foil is in the drawer on the other side of the sink."

"Sure, Miss Laine." He grinned down at his employer. "I told you she'd be impossible to push around."

On that note, Dennis and Drew left. She locked gazes with her friend and mentor.

"All right," he huffed after a long moment. "So we should have asked first."

"Thank you," she said. "Why didn't you ask? You of all people know better than to try the heavy-handed act on me."

"I was afraid you might balk at the idea of Drew covering for you."

"Good heavens, why would you think that?"

"Because he's pushy. Comes by it naturally," he admitted wryly. "And because you and he weren't getting

along at the office there at first. And—" his face red-
dened with controlled anger "—that's the second time
I've seen him making a pass at you. If he's been taking
advantage of you, I swear I'll—"

"Hold it right there," she said, getting to her feet,
then standing in front of him. "You calm down and I
will tell you exactly how things are. I will take this vacation because it's what I want. And if you had asked,
I would have agreed without any fuss."

"Good. Then everything's settled."

"Not so fast. About what you saw a few moments
ago. You will not say anything to Drew. Arthur, he's
been taking care of me these past few days. I know you
want to protect me—"

"You're the daughter I always wanted to have."

She knelt down and took his old hands in hers. "I
love you dearly. You've been wonderful to me and to
Cody. But Arthur, where does Drew figure into your
feelings?"

"I love him. You know that."

She sighed. "You know and I know. Half of Kansas
City knows. But I'm not sure Drew does."

The old man's brow wrinkled. "What do you
mean?"

"You're always on his case."

"I want him to be..."

"What?" she prompted when he remained quiet.
"He's talented, successful, respected and admired—"

"But sometimes he's so cold and distant. He doesn't
seem to have a lot of close friends."

"I don't think that kind of closeness comes easily for
him, so he keeps people at a distance. Maybe to protect
himself. But, believe me, he isn't cold at all."

Arthur studied her thoughtfully. "So what's going on between you two?"

"Nothing right now."

"Nothing? What I saw didn't look like nothing."

Laine smiled a bit self-consciously. "Well, just a kiss now and then. But—" she pointed a warning finger at him "—you stay out of it until one or the other of us asks for your opinion. If you have to talk to Drew, tell him how you feel about him."

He shifted in his chair. "Laine, I can talk to you. You make it so easy. But with Drew . . . The trouble is, I'm not sure he wants to hear it. Maybe there was a time, once, but . . ."

She stood and leaned down to kiss his cheek as the screen door opened and Drew and Dennis came out. "Talk to him," she said in Arthur's ear.

"Well, I don't see any blood shed," Dennis remarked.

Drew stiffened his spine, and balancing the tray in one hand placed the other possessively on Laine's shoulder. He refused to let the old man's wrath keep him from taking care of her.

"You should be taking it easy," he said firmly as he led her back to the swing.

"Lucky for you, I agree," she replied with her lilting laughter. "How much longer before you put the steaks on?" she asked as he positioned the foil-wrapped potatoes and ears of corn over the coals.

"About thirty minutes or so," he said.

"That's where this comes in." Dennis handed her a platter of crackers, sliced cheeses, carrots and celery sticks. "Mr. Drew had me fix this now because he said you were hungry."

Arthur watched the exchange with interest, Drew noted, but his glower was gone. What had Laine said to the old man? He put the last ear of corn on the grill, then sat next to her.

She smiled at him. "So what are we doing next week?" she asked, passing him the platter. "Since I'm on vacation."

"You said you have a long list of things Cody will need for his trip to SPACE CAMP. I figured I'd leave the office around noon and we can tackle that first."

"I want to give him some spending money," Arthur insisted. "The camp fee must have cost him practically everything he's saved since Christmas."

Laine nodded. "He insisted on paying for the whole thing himself, so I'm sure he'll appreciate a little pocket money."

Just then the subject of their conversation came running around the side of the house. "Hi, Mom. Hi, everybody," Cody said breathlessly. "I saw Arthur's car in the driveway, so I rushed home. Is dinner ready yet?"

Camped out on the living room couch, Laine listened to Cody and Drew talk in the kitchen as they cleaned up after dinner. If she held her head just right she could keep Drew in her line of vision and feast her eyes on the sight of him. Every time he moved, his shoulders stretched under his knit shirt. His sleeves were rolled up, providing her starving sight with constant glimpses of his forearms. She tried to concentrate on his wrists—thinking she would be safe there—but her thoughts only drifted to his powerful hands and she was lost in wanting to feel them caressing her.

Again she felt the ache of desire that had been growing steadily from their first moments together, and gaining strength since he'd brought her home ill. More than once this weekend she'd imagined what it would be like to have him become part of their lives—hers and Cody's. At first she'd thought it was a fairy-tale wish, that it could never come true, and wishing for what couldn't be would only destroy her peace of mind. But lately she'd begun to reconsider. She thought she wanted Drew in her life and knew she wanted him to make love to her.

Once the last dish was put away and Cody had said good-night, Drew sat beside her on the couch.

"I believe," he said in a low and dangerously seductive voice, "that before our company interrupted us, I was making some promises as to the things I would do if you took next week off work."

"I've already agreed," she said, trembling with longing and excitement as he pulled her into his embrace. "But, Drew, I think we might be moving too fast."

He pulled her onto his lap, but when she expected him to press his advantage, he just laid her head on his shoulder and held her.

"Occasionally I think we're rushing things, too," he said softly. "Then I start wanting you so much I can't think clearly."

"So what do we do?"

Drew sighed. "Enjoy next week. We'll talk about it some more, then. Meanwhile, I ought to leave before I change my mind and decide rushing's not such a bad thing."

But he made no effort to move. She felt so right in his arms. He let the ecstasy of the moment crowd out all the doubts and fears. Her breasts rose and fell with her breathing, brushing his chest, making him almost mindless with need.

"What are you going to do while Cody's at SPACE CAMP?" he asked her in order to divert his thoughts.

She chuckled. "Paint his room."

Drew groaned. "Laine, you can't tackle projects like that by yourself."

"Of course I can, Mr. Overprotective Smothering Male."

"Then at least let me help."

"You'll still be in Kansas City?"

"I'll stay just for that."

"I don't know," she said thoughtfully. "The last time we tried painting something, we ended up having a water fight one day and throwing paint at each other the next."

"Just imagine what might happen when we're alone with no child to interrupt."

He could feel her tense on his lap and knew exactly the direction her mind had taken. That he had the power to make her want him was a heady feeling, unlike anything he'd ever known.

He stood her on her feet and tilted her chin up. Her eyes burned with a desire he wanted to unleash, but would the fire end up destroying them both?

He gently kissed her goodbye and left.

When the door closed, Laine let out the breath she'd been holding. She'd thought he was going to take her to bed then and there, and she'd wanted him to do just that. Only that. Regardless of the consequences.

Just as she'd wanted him to make love to her for so many nights now. Each moment she was with him, she vividly recalled the kisses they'd shared. Often she would catch his gaze on her and note the heat in his eyes that indicated he, too, was remembering.

Her frustration was getting the better of her. Alone in her room, she tossed and turned in her full-size bed, longing to feel the warmth of him lying next to her. She slept for a while, then awakened with dreams of making love with him fresh in her mind, quickening her heartbeat.

She fluffed her pillow and lay staring at the darkened ceiling, thinking of Drew. The man was changing her life, day by wonderful day. He made her imagine the future—the same future she'd dreamed of as a young woman. Children and a husband who was both her lover and her best friend. Now that mysterious man had a name. Drew.

Earlier tonight he'd all but said they would make love once Cody had left for camp. She realized now that he'd been giving her time to get used to the idea, time to decide exactly where she wanted their relationship to go. This was further evidence of how deep his caring went. He knew making love was not something she would take lightly.

But how much of a commitment was he willing to make? She didn't want a long-distance romance. She'd been alone far too many years, bearing the burdens herself. She wanted someone by her side, not a disembodied voice over the phone wires. Someone she could see, hold, touch. Someone to lie next to at night, to fill those dark hours with passion and love, to share her soul's secrets.

She wanted someone willing to open his heart and soul to her in return. She would have the next two weeks before Cody left for camp to learn if Drew could be that man.

Chapter Eleven

"**T**raveling!" Cody shouted. "She's traveling. Did you see that?"

Laine came to a dead stop, basketball in her hands, exasperation written on her face. "You guys do it all the time."

Drew grinned, figuring he could guess where she was headed with her argument.

Cody looked offended. "We do not."

"Sure, you do. You just do it so fast it can't be detected. It is humanly impossible to bounce this ball the entire time you're walking or running downcourt."

Drew laughed, something he'd done a lot of this past week. "You bounce it once for every step you take." He took the ball from her and tried a slow-motion demonstration.

"Just proves you're not human," she grumbled as he walked a circle around her.

"Funny." He stopped behind her, reaching around to dribble the ball in front of her feet.

Dangerous move, he thought, getting a whiff of her delicate perfume. This was the fourth day of her vacation and each day tested his control more than the one before. He'd spent as little time as possible at the office and as much time as he could with her—and Cody.

They'd done the Kansas City Museum and the Nelson-Atkins and the Baseball Hall of Fame. They'd picnicked at Loose Park, strolling hand in hand through the Rose Garden while Cody walked ahead, then fed the ducks down at the pond. They'd gone to the movies and the mall, the grocery store and dry cleaner's. He'd even sat in the doctor's waiting room when she'd taken Cody for his precamp physical. It hadn't mattered where he was, as long as he was with her.

"Okay, Mr. Basketball," she said. "You can dribble with the best of them."

Drew chuckled but kept on dribbling the basketball in front of her. She stepped to the right, so did he. She moved to the left, he moved with her. She tried to knock the ball away from him, he managed to elude her hands.

Cody applauded his speed and skill. Finally Laine whirled around to face Drew. Her small breasts brushed his arms.

Drew wished he and Laine were alone and gave thanks they weren't. He would have kissed her. Wouldn't have been able to stop himself. His blood raced through his body and his heart pounded in his ears.

"Shopping," Laine finally gasped. It was the only word she could get out to break the spell created by the bright heat in his eyes. He was much too close and oh, so far away. She should push him away, but she only wanted to pull him closer.

"Shopping is not what I want to do," he said, his voice as low and seductive as one of his kisses.

"We going to the mall now?" Cody asked excitedly. He bounced the ball hard on the driveway. It hit a crack in the pavement and rebounded to Drew who caught it and twirled it on the tip of his finger.

"I guess we are," he said to Cody. If we can't do what we really want to do, his eyes said to Laine.

"Great! I can't wait to get those new basketball shoes. I'm ready now. All I have to do is change my shirt." Cody raced into the house.

"I suppose I should change, too," Drew commented, walking her to the front door.

Laine longed to protest that he shouldn't change a thing. He'd worked up a healthy sweat in the warm early-afternoon sun, and the dampness had molded his T-shirt to his muscled torso. Those gym shorts left little to her overactive imagination.... Watching him with Cody those brief moments before they'd dragged her into the game, she'd decided how the power and strength in his legs would feel as he made love to her.

In the kitchen he gave her a quick peck on the cheek, then went to her bedroom to get his clothes. His things were scattered all over the downstairs—clothing on the chair in the bedroom, toiletries in the bathroom, shoes in the living room, a couple more neckties on the coat-rack by the kitchen door, his fax machine scrunched into a corner of her desk and business papers littering the coffee table. Although he went to Arthur's every night, he always managed to leave something behind.

She liked seeing Drew's things in her house, she'd decided that first weekend when he nursed her back to health. Everything about his being a part of her life had become wonderfully comfortable. As he walked back into the kitchen, his sweat-dampened hair freshly combed, his fitted jeans riding low on his lean hips and the fire in his eyes only slightly banked, she knew he was the missing piece in her life.

He caged her at the sink, his long hard body pressing into hers, his mouth against her ear. "Hey, sexy mama. Where's the kid?"

On cue, Cody's footsteps thundered on the stairs. Drew smiled at her, so much loving warmth in his gaze that it took her breath away.

Cody bounded into the kitchen and stopped. "What are you guys doing?" he asked, his young brow furrowed.

Drew's grin widened, but he didn't move away. Instead he reached around her and snatched a glass out of the cabinet. "Just getting a drink," he said, filling the glass from the tap behind her.

"I could move out of your way," she offered, a smile of her own tugging at the corners of her mouth.

"Not on your life," he said so only she could hear.

Impossible as it was, having him pressed against her this way was torture and ecstasy both. Gazing up into his devilishly sexy grin, she knew this was the side of him she treasured the most—a touch of playful humor mixed with a ton of erotic promise.

Gradually she remembered her son was watching the exchange with an extraordinary amount of interest. Drew must have realized it, too. He drained the glass of water and set it on the counter as he stepped away from her. But long after that, his heat stayed with her.

* * *

Cody was laughing so hard he could barely breathe. His friend, Buzzie, had come over for a game of hoops and some pointers. Drew had given the tips, done a little coaching and Cody now literally ran circles around the other boy, who stood frozen in disbelief at his skill.

"Wow!" he finally managed. "Can you teach me how to do it that fast?"

"Practice," Cody said knowingly.

"That's the key," Drew said with a deep sense of pride that Cody had adopted his advice.

This was Sunday, the last day of their vacation together. He couldn't remember ever being this happy, contented, or peaceful. He felt a part of a whole—something he hadn't felt in a very long time.

He showed the two boys a few more moves, then Buzzie's mom called him to come home.

"So, show me how much good the hand weights have done you," Drew said, turning the ball over to Cody.

The boy made several shots, the accuracy of which clearly indicated improvement in his control. Drew suggested another couple of exercises that would help further, then the two of them went to weed the garden as they'd promised Laine.

"What about karate lessons?" Cody asked, taking a whack at a fairly sizable weed. "One of my friends is taking a class that starts after the Fourth of July."

"You want me to work on your mom while you're gone?" He grinned when Cody nodded. "I suppose I did say I'd help talk her into it."

"If you don't mind, I mean."

He didn't mind. In fact, he genuinely liked how Cody turned to him for advice and support. It made him feel like he belonged, even if it was only for a while.

"It was fun trying to teach Mom to play basketball the other day, wasn't it?"

Drew nodded. Fun had never been a big part of his life until now. There just hadn't been room for it. And when he really thought about it, what made doing things fun was being with the people he was close to.

"Heck, even painting the house was fun," Cody continued. "The water fight... Man, that was awesome."

Drew had to chuckle. "I've had a great time this week."

"Even taking care of Mom when she was sick?"

Drew bent his head over a weed to hide a smile. "Yeah, I even enjoyed that." Enjoyed being needed. Enjoyed having her trust him and depend on him the way she had, knowing that he'd eased her aches and pains. Best of all, enjoyed that the wonder of being with her had lasted through the week.

"So, I was wondering," Cody said hesitantly. "I mean, can I ask you something? You don't have to answer if you can't or don't want to."

Drew glanced up, a brow raised inquiringly. "What is it, Cody?"

"Well, it's about Mom."

"What about her?"

"Well, it's kind of about you...."

"Me?" Drew asked, aware of a tightening in his gut at the feeling Cody was heading where he didn't want to go.

"Kind of. It's about you and Mom, I guess. You know, the two of you."

Drew straightened, cold fear gripping his insides.

"I mean, I've seen you guys holding hands and I think maybe a couple of times you might have been kissing her."

"Cody..." He had to set the boy straight—put things back into their proper perspective for the kid. For himself, too.

"Then there was the time you guys were fighting and painted each other and then you made up."

"Cody..." He tried again, but the words he had to say stuck in his throat.

"So, anyway," Cody rushed on, "I wondered if you were going to marry Mom."

Drew stood frozen, unable to move as shock shot through him, painfully intense. How could he have been so irresponsible to have let matters go this far? How could he have ignored the signs, not realized the boy had seen them together and read more into the situation than was meant?

He hadn't been thinking past the present moment, but Cody had been planning far into the future. He'd never wanted to hurt the kid, hated that he would have to do so now, but Cody was hoping for more than Drew could give.

To pretend that what they all shared now might outlast the summer would be the ultimate cruelty. *Long-term* and *forever after* were words that never had and never would apply to him, Drew thought bitterly.

He turned to face the boy squarely. "Marriage is not something to rush into. It's an important step. One your mom and I aren't ready to take."

"But I thought— I mean, the way you took care of her when she was sick..."

"Your mom needed someone. She's a very special person."

"But you don't love her." Disappointment laced his words.

"Not that way," Drew said gently, then realized just what a lie that was.

He loved her. Completely. She was all he'd ever longed for. And if he dared to reach for it, this wonderful thing he'd found with her would turn sour. Somehow, some way, it would all fall apart. And this time he wouldn't be able to pick up the pieces.

Love didn't last for him. If only he could find the words to make Cody understand.

"I like being with her," he tried to explain. "I like talking to her, laughing, having fun, even holding her hand and sometimes kissing her."

"But isn't that what love is?"

"There are different degrees. One day you'll start looking at girls as more than pests. Then you'll understand. Some girls you'll like a little, they're fun to be around. Some girls you'll like a lot, they're fun to be around and you're attracted to them. Some girls will be special and one girl you'll fall in love with and want to marry."

Drew had found his one girl at last, but the happiness he wanted couldn't be for him. He hoped Cody would never have to suffer that pain.

"Does Mom know how you feel?" he asked with his usual readiness to protect Laine.

Drew nodded, but as soon as he did, he had to wonder if she, like Cody, had been hoping for more from him...more than he could give. He'd let them all down.

They weeded the rest of the garden in silence, then carried the tools into the garage. Cody studied the hoe he'd set against the back wall, then turned to Drew. The look in his eyes demanded a truth Drew didn't want to give, but couldn't dodge.

"You're really not going to marry Mom?"

Drew shook his head. "My company is in Dallas and I have to go back and take care of business. I'll have enough work to catch up on to keep me busy for months, and there'll be more work after that."

"But you've been in Kansas City all this time."

"Because Arthur needed me, and then your mom was sick, and she needed a short vacation and she wouldn't worry about the office if I was here."

And he hadn't been able to stay away. He'd needed to be here with her as much as he needed air to breathe. She'd become that essential. What would he do without the sunshine of her smile to warm his cold and lonely soul?

"So you're going back to Dallas, then?" Cody asked.

Drew nodded. "That was always the plan."

He was taking the coward's way out, Drew realized as he packed for the trip home. But he needed time to assess the damage he'd done. Needed to start easing into this separation. For everyone's sake.

There was a slight rap on his half-open bedroom door, then Emma Jenkins came in carrying some folded, freshly ironed shirts. "You still have a couple of suits at the cleaner's," she told him. "What do you want me to do with them when they come back?"

"Leave them in this closet. I'll pick them up on my next trip through. I left some things over at Laine's, too. Ask Dennis to stop by her house tomorrow evening and get them."

He hadn't been able to face Laine. Hell, he hadn't even gone into the house to say he was leaving. A lousy way to handle the situation. He owed her more than that. But he couldn't have stood seeing the censure and contempt in her eyes, though it was no more than he deserved; couldn't have lived with himself if he'd seen the slightest trace of pain there.

Damn! He'd made a first-class mess of things. Couldn't have botched it better if he'd tried. He laid the last two shirts in the suitcase, shut it, then straightened as he heard the whir of Arthur's electric wheelchair.

The old man watched him lift the suitcase off the bed and set it on the floor. "This is rather sudden, isn't it?"

"Emergency. I'll be in Minneapolis for a week or so," Drew said, hoping, praying, the old man didn't ask too many questions. The truth was he didn't have business in Minneapolis. Didn't have business anywhere other than Kansas City, but it was business he couldn't deal with. Not yet. Maybe not ever. Minneapolis was no more than a place to hole up for a while and sort things out in his mind.

"What about Laine?" Arthur asked, getting right to the point, to the matter of the person most important to him. Most important to Drew, as well.

"She'll be able to run things with your superintendent's help in the field and you here to guide them."

"That's not what I mean and you know it," Arthur growled. "You haven't told her you're leaving, have you?"

There was no explanation he could give that his uncle would accept, Drew was sure. "It's better this way."

"You led her on, then you sneak out like a thief in the night and say it's better this way. You're no nephew of mine."

How that cut! "I never was, was I?"

Drew slung his garment-bag strap over his shoulder, grabbed his suitcase and was halfway down the hall when Arthur's voice boomed at him. "What the hell is that supposed to mean?"

Time to clear the air, Drew decided as he turned to face the other man. "You were never there for me. When I needed you most, you quit asking me to visit, quit phoning, never had much to say when I called."

"You don't understand," Arthur said, his voice strained.

"Not completely. I've always supposed that since the visits and calls stopped after Mom's death, it had something to do with how much I look like her."

"You have her eyes, her black hair, her smile at times." He wheeled his chair a few inches closer, then stopped. "Ann was my baby sister. Our parents—your grandparents—were old by the time she came along. I taught her how to tie her shoes, how to dance, how to drive. Everything. Every time I looked at you, I missed her unbearably."

"I remember you were close. But, damn it, I loved her, too." As the long-pent-up words came out, so did the hurt and confusion of that lost little boy he'd been. "I needed you and Dad."

Arthur sighed heavily. "We should have all pulled together instead of going our separate ways. By the time I pulled myself out of my sorrow, you were so distant. I figured it was too late. Maybe it still is...."

Arthur studied him intently, waiting, his frail hands tight on the arms of his chair. The old man had locked him out and was now asking, begging, for another chance.

"It isn't too late," Drew said, knowing it might have been—had he walked out, had Arthur not stopped him.

Arthur exhaled heavily. "We can't change the past, but we do have the future."

The older man had done the best he could, dealing with his own pain over his sister's death. Drew sympathized and accepted that. What he couldn't accept, though, were all those years they'd lost. Important years. Years they could never get back. If only one of them had put aside his pride enough to say something to change the situation before now.

The grandfather clock in the library chimed ten o'clock. "I've got to go," Drew said. "I'll be back."

Arthur wheeled up to his nephew. "Drew, I never stopped caring about you."

The words he'd needed to hear for so very long. Drew slowly dropped his luggage, then bent over the wheelchair to hug his uncle.

"What about Laine?" Arthur asked again.

"Things never really got started between us. It's better if I leave now before they do." But how the hell was he going to make it without her?

Chapter Twelve

Drew was gone. Out of her life as suddenly as he'd come into it. He hadn't even wanted to say goodbye to her. Laine would have been furious but the hurt kept crowding it out.

Over and over she mentally replayed their last day together. They'd gone to church, out to brunch and the movies. They'd bought the paint for Cody's bedroom and had made plans to paint it together.

Something had happened to make him change his mind about being with her, about making love to her.

"If you're not going to eat that salmon steak, at least don't maul it," Arthur said sharply. "It's expensive."

Laine looked across the dining room table at him. She was trying to hide how empty she felt, and she'd almost succeeded the first day or two. Until she'd somehow deleted the Accounts Receivable year-to-date transaction history from the computer. The third day, Cody had come in from an after-dinner basketball practice at Buzzie's and caught her crying. This was the fourth day since Drew had left and she'd given up trying to hide how bereft she felt.

She laid her fork on the plate and her napkin on the table, then pushed her chair back. "I'm going for a walk in the gardens," she told Arthur and Cody.

Sitting on a stone bench in the rose garden, she could see the garage and the basketball goal. So many memories, so many ghosts to haunt her dreams and walk beside her during the days.

She'd known Drew for three short weeks and in that time they'd shared so much. She'd first thought he was a tyrant, but had learned he wasn't anything like her father or her ex-husband. She could deal with him, reason with him, laugh with him, and love him. More than she'd ever thought it possible to love a man.

She'd thought they were growing close. But she'd been so wrong, and was paying a heavy price for having dared to hope. She had wanted him to be the man for her, wanted it so much.

"So how long are you going to sit out here?"

Laine started at the sound of Arthur's sharp voice. She'd been so lost in thought, she hadn't heard his wheelchair; hadn't noticed evening had turned to dusk.

"I didn't realize it was getting dark," she said wearily.

"You haven't noticed anything at all these last few days," he stated in a tight voice. Then the control quickly snapped. "Damn that boy's hide!"

Laine whirled to face him. "Drew is not responsible for how I feel. I won't allow you to blame him."

"He hurt you."

She sighed. "Leaving without saying goodbye, yes. But that's all he has to answer for. He never broke any promises." Because he'd been very careful not to make any, she now realized.

She had no one but herself to blame for the way she'd let her longings run wild. She'd let herself think he truly cared for her, that he might love her—just because he'd been so warm and tender, because he'd stayed with her that night her head throbbed and her body hurt with fever. He'd been kind and wonderful and giving, but he'd never once said anything about love.

Arthur came closer to take her hand in his. "Laine..."

She laid her other hand along the side of his face. "I'll be all right," she said, though she didn't see how she could go through the rest of her life with this unbearable pain in her soul. "I just need a little time."

Arthur nodded, though doubt shone in his eyes. When she took her hands away and folded them in her lap, he sighed. "This is my fault," he said.

"How? Because I asked you not to say anything to him and you didn't?" She forced a small smile for his benefit.

The smile he gave her in return held a lot of regret. "He thinks I deserted him when Ann died. And I did."

"He talked to you?" Laine asked, glad that the two men had started to communicate with each other.

"It was less a case of talking and more a case of telling me off," Arthur admitted wryly. "But now I understand that if he was cold and distant, it was because he figured I didn't care."

"That's a start," Laine said, sadness stealing over her again. She'd thought she and Drew had begun something rare and wonderful, but he hadn't told her he planned on leaving. Hadn't even said goodbye. Hadn't shared his feelings with her.

That's what it all boiled down to. He'd taken this monumental step, severing their relationship, and he hadn't seen the need to discuss it with her. How could she have misread him so completely?

"It's late," she said, getting to her feet.

Arthur nodded, not saying anything as she walked him inside, still silent as she collected Cody and the two of them left. There was nothing to say.

As soon as she pulled the car into the garage, Cody sprinted into the house. By the time Laine walked in, he was coming out of her bedroom, his arms laden with clothing, a pair of shoes, and toiletries.

Drew's things, she realized, catching sight of the striped tie that had hung on her bedpost all this time. Cody dumped the things on the floor, then went into the kitchen and returned with the ties that Drew had left hanging by the door and a trash bag.

"Cody, what are you doing?" she asked in alarm, looking at the things she hadn't been able to pack up. That would have been more final than she could have dealt with.

"I don't want his stuff here," Cody grumbled as he began shoving clothes into the bag. "I'm going to set them out for the trash. I hate him."

"Cody," Laine gasped. "Don't say that."

"I do. I hate him. And I hate these!" In a flash, he yanked off the basketball shoes Drew had bought him and threw them into the bag.

"Cody—"

"He made you cry. He told me that you would understand, that you would be okay when he went back to Dallas, but you're not."

Laine opened her arms and pulled Cody into her embrace. Despite all his brave anger, he burst into tears.

She held him, her young would-be protector. Being without Drew was so painful for her that she hadn't thought about what Cody was going through.

"It's my fault he left," Cody said through his tears.

"Your fault?" First Arthur and now Cody trying to take the blame.

"I asked him if he was going to marry you. That's when he told me he had to go."

One of the puzzle pieces snapped into place. "Slugger, what else did he say?"

"That you were special. I saw you guys kissing and holding hands. He said he liked being around you. So maybe he left because of me."

Laine led her son over to the couch and sat beside him. "No, Cody, it had nothing to do with you. He liked you. A lot. And he ... liked ... me."

"Then why did he leave?"

"I think it was because he was afraid of loving us."

Afraid because he'd loved and lost so many times before. Now it made sense that he hadn't been able to stay when Cody brought up the subject of marriage.

But by the same token, if he'd been so frightened that he'd had to run from her, didn't that mean he cared?

Drew set his suitcases and garment bag on the living room floor and glanced around his condo. Home. The place had never seemed more lonely. But without Laine, the emptiness was everywhere.

He hadn't been able to escape it. Not the week in Minneapolis where he'd had nothing to do but think of her and beat himself up for forgetting all the lessons love had taught him. Not in Atlanta where he'd spent two days looking over the work Jake Tanner was doing there. Not here where the silence surrounded him and the memories overtook him.

Like now, looking at the three ties draped over the arm of his sofa. The striped one he'd wrapped around her bedpost the night she was so ill with the flu. The navy one with the tiny red diamond pattern that she'd admired. The gray one with the splashes of muted mauve tones. She'd bought that one for him. It was too modern for his conservative tastes, but when he'd arrived the next morning with it on and she'd walked up to straighten it, she'd smiled up at him with so much love in her gaze.

He'd left that tie and the others at her house, but the memories were so vivid he could almost believe the ties were really there. Could almost believe those were really her things in his living room—her sandals on the floor by the coffee table, her purse on the table beside the wing chair, her dark green linen jacket hanging from the back of the dining room chair.

The unreal images summed up his life quite well—a bunch of unfulfilled longings. Before Laine, those wishes and wants had been vague, unfocused. Now he knew that all he needed and couldn't have was her.

A noise in the kitchen made him slowly lift his head. He turned to see her walk out, looking as real as the other things he'd imagined there. He was too exhausted from endless nights without sleep to blink away the image of her in the semidarkness, backlit by the kitchen night-light. Besides, it was nearly one in the morning—the time when he couldn't keep the ghosts at bay.

But tonight the apparition wasn't wearing that flowered sundress she'd finished sewing their last week together. Her dark green slacks matched the jacket on the chair and the bright colors in her sleeveless blouse would bring out the gold in her lovely eyes. And this time the apparition carried something on a plate—a sandwich, he realized as she switched on the dining room light and set the plate on the table.

"I thought you might be hungry," she said.

He hadn't realized how starved he was for the sound of her voice. But he hung back, certain this vision would vanish if he moved. Laine couldn't be here. Not after the way he'd treated her.

He'd hurt her badly. He knew, because Arthur hadn't mentioned her once during their daily phone conversations. If she'd been fine, Arthur would have told him. The fact that he hadn't said a word about her meant the subject was too painful to discuss.

"I'm sorry," he whispered. "I never meant to hurt you."

"I know," she answered, her voice husky with emotion. "It took me a while, but I finally decided that's something you would never do. I also figured out you wouldn't come to me."

She walked toward him. Drew's breath caught. Never in any of his midnight conversations with this vision had she spoken her forgiveness—only her contempt. And never had she walked toward him. Only away.

Laine stopped in front of him, taking in the generous stubble, his rumpled suit and missing tie. There was such confusion in his gaze, and when he looked down into her eyes, she felt as if she were seeing into his very soul. A soul as tortured as her own.

"Oh, Drew." She placed her palm along his cheek.

He started at her touch, caught her wrist, then studied her hand for a long moment. "You're here? Really here?" His eyes narrowed. "But why?"

She wanted to smooth away the deep lines of fatigue that furrowed his brow, but there was much that had to be settled first. "I have to know why you left the way you did."

"I had to."

Laine felt her shaky courage falter. Coming here had been the biggest risk of her life and she'd had to fight the urge to play it safe, tuck tail and run. She'd convinced herself that if she could just get him started talking to her, they might have a chance. Now she wasn't so sure.

"You owe me more than that," she said.

"It's all I can give you." With a heavy sigh, he sank down onto the sofa.

She saw her hopes slipping further away. He wasn't going to try to meet her halfway.

"You haven't asked how I got in," she said, forcing a conversational tone when she wanted to cry, or scream at him, plead with him.

He placed his head in his hands. Just when she thought she'd lost him completely, he raised it.

"I figure you got security to let you in," he said. "Though I don't know how you talked Frank into it."

"I told him we were getting married," she explained, half holding her breath as she waited for his reaction.

He stared at her for a long moment, then laughed humorlessly. "And he believed you?"

"As a matter of fact, he said he figured you were involved with someone out of town because you travel so much and haven't had a woman up to this apartment in a year and a half."

His brow quirked ever so slightly, a ghost of that old familiar arch that used to infuriate her no end. But that was the only response he gave.

"Drew," she said softly, "we have to talk."

"I can't."

She'd never thought two simple words could be so frightening to hear, but they were.

"You talked to me that night in my bedroom," she said, reaching past her fear to find her anger. How could he let what they shared go so easily? "Maybe it only works when I'm sick. Is that it?"

His only reply was another deep sigh.

"Well, okay. If that's the case . . . I can't get ill every time we have to talk, but if it'll get things started this time. . ." She flopped down next to him on the sofa and threw her arm over her forehead melodramatically. "Oh, I feel so lousy."

"Laine," he said wearily, "you're being ridiculous."

"I know. But if this is what it takes, I'm prepared to be ill as long as necessary."

"You can't stay here that long," he argued in the same lifeless tone. "What about Cody?"

"He's at camp the rest of this week, and if I need to stay longer, Arthur will take care of him. For as long as necessary. Till he graduates from high school, if need be. I can be as stubborn as you."

"This isn't about stubbornness."

"Sure, it is. I want to know why you walked out on us and you won't tell me. That's stubborn in my book."

His shoulders slumped. He started to get up. She couldn't let him walk away again. She snatched up the gray tie and whipped it around his neck and pulled.

With a strangled cough, he sank back against the cushions. She quickly straddled his lap.

"Laine," he gasped, trying to slide a finger under the tie.

She loosened her hold on the ends—slightly. "I knew these things would come in handy," she mused aloud. "I just didn't know what for."

"You nearly choked me," he croaked.

"Yeah, well, I'll hang you with it if you don't start talking to me."

He caught her upper arms, his hold unyielding. There was a flash of desperate determination in his eyes. It sparked her hope that she could somehow reach him.

"That's it," she encouraged, as his eyes began to blaze with the heat she remembered. She tried to lean closer, but he held her at bay.

"What are you doing?" he growled.

"Trying anything I can think of to get past that defeatist attitude of yours. You never let anything hold you back in business, so why are you giving up on us?"

"Don't do this." It was part command and part plea.

"Don't tell you that I love you? Don't say that living without you has been sheer hell? Well, it's all true. And I'm not leaving here until I know why you think you can waltz into my life, make me fall in love with you, then waltz out without even a pretty please."

Drew groaned. "I didn't want you to fall in love with me anymore than I wanted to fall in love with you. Love doesn't last. Not for me."

She jerked on the ends of the tie, hard enough to make him cough.

"What's that for?" he demanded when he could talk.

"You! Love doesn't last for you," she scoffed. "Nothing lasts if you don't fight to keep it!"

She threw her arms around his neck and kissed him with all the emotion that thrummed through her slender frame. Drew could feel it all and couldn't resist his own need for her. He'd been without her for so long, empty and alone. She was the light of his life and without her, all was darkness.

He wrapped his arms around her, pressing her to him, feeling her life pour into him. He needed her with a desperation deeper than anything he'd ever known. He drank greedily of her sweetness and felt it heal his wounded soul.

But still that moment of reckoning lurked in the recesses of his mind. He wound his fingers through the silk of her hair and gently pulled her away.

"Laine, you're not hearing what I've said." He saw the tears in her eyes and felt his heart break. "I can't go through this pain again. One day you would want to leave me and I wouldn't be able to survive this time."

She sniffed. "I can't promise our lives would be perfect."

"Sweetheart, look at what you have to go through to get me to talk to you. It will never be easy for you."

"But it's not impossible. I can always fake an illness or threaten to hang you with your own ties."

"You may get very tired of that."

"I'm hoping that in twenty-five or thirty years I'll be able to convince you to trust me."

"Will you be serious for just a minute," he snapped.

"I am." She blinked and one tear trailed down her cheek. "Drew, I want to be there for you, the way you were there for me. I know there might be a time when there's something you won't want to share with me and I'll try to respect that. But if something involves us, we have to talk about it."

"This is so important to you and so difficult for me," he said. "I'm afraid I'll let you down. You or Cody."

She laughed a little, then lowered her mouth to his ear. "Don't look now, but you're talking to me. And I don't think it's as painful as you're making it out to be."

She was going to drive him crazy, Drew thought. Happily crazy. But did he dare take another chance on love? She nipped his earlobe and suddenly he knew that no matter what problems the future might hold, he couldn't go through life without her.

She wanted him enough to chase him down and make him see reason. She loved him enough to fight for him. She wouldn't leave him. If there was something about their relationship she didn't like, she would get her back up and go to war. But she wouldn't desert him.

Somehow Laine found herself lying flat on her back on the couch, Drew leaning over her, the leer in his eyes leaving no doubt as to how the rest of the night would be spent.

"I suppose I should *ask* you to marry me," he said, his voice holding a hint of laughter and all the love she could hope for. "Just so we don't have the complications we had over the vacation."

"Might be a good idea."

He began trailing long, lingering kisses down the column of her beautiful neck. "Will you marry me? Be my wife, my best friend, my lover?"

"And perhaps the mother of your children?"

He raised his head and stared down at her. He'd given up the idea of a family of his own when Caro had refused to have his baby. "Children," he said, savoring the word. "Would you . . ."

She smiled up at him. "Yes. I want you. I want to marry you and have everything that goes with it. The good, the bad, and the kids. Now, I think you left off right about here." She pointed to a spot just below where her pulse beat strong and hard.

He resumed, making his way down the open vee of her blouse, stopping at the first button. He moaned at the tiny glimpse of cleavage there. Her delicate scent surrounded him, the very perfume that had taunted and tantalized him the first time they met. As the conflicting needs to rush and savor battled within him, he decided to share them with her.

"I can't decide whether I want to rip this blouse off you or undress you slow enough to make it last all night," he said in her ear.

In that moment, Laine knew that whatever the future held for them, they would make it. "If I have any say in the matter," she managed, her heart swelling with love for him, "I opt for the first choice."

He captured her arms, raised them over her head and held them there. "I've decided on making it last," he told her. "We'll do it your way next time."

"Why, you overbearing, dominating, macho male." She sighed as he undid the first button, then slowly bent his head to nuzzle the cleavage he'd uncovered.

"I've needed you for so long," he said against her skin. "All my life." The second button soon gave way, then the third.

Hours later Laine lay in Drew's bed, his arms around her, her head cradled in the hollow of his shoulder. They'd made love there on the sofa—more hurriedly than Drew had planned because once he'd touched her, he'd wanted her more than his willpower could withstand—then more slowly here in his bed.

"I suppose we should call Arthur in the morning," he said around a yawn.

"Mmm."

"Speaking of the old man, who's minding the office?"

"You don't want to know."

"Crissie." He groaned. "Oh, well, I suppose she'll be okay for one day."

"Actually, more like three."

"What?"

"Or more, depending on how long you want to stay in Dallas."

"Laine," he growled, "what are you talking about?"

"I've been here for two days already, waiting for you to decide to come home. Three tomorrow. And I told Arthur I wasn't coming back without you." She patted his chest reassuringly. "But not to worry. She can't mess up anything. I pretty much managed to wipe out most of the stuff on the computer this past week."

"How the hell— Never mind. I don't want to talk about Arthur's office or computer problems right now."

She was running her fingers through the hair on his chest and it must have been having the effect she wanted because when she angled her head to look up at him, the heat of his gaze, burned her with its intensity.

"What about your company?" she ventured. She still didn't want a long-distance romance, but she would take whatever he could give her just to be with him.

"I was thinking about that when I carried you in here. Corporate headquarters should be located where it's most beneficial for the company. I figure that's Kansas City."

"Really? You would move your company?"

"Arthur needs you in that office and I need you with me. I don't want you to have to decide between me and Arthur, and now that I've found you, I'm not coming home at night to an empty apartment and an empty bed. Is that too selfish for you?"

"In this case, selfish is good."

"What about Cody? How do you think he'll take to us getting married?"

She laughed. "You may have a few fences to mend."

"He's upset because I hurt you."

"Basically. But I don't think you'll have a lot of trouble smoothing things over with him. He pretty much worships the ground you dribble a basketball on."

Drew's arms tightened possessively around her. "Did I mention that I love you?"

"Yes, but feel free to say it often. And I will remind you that I love you, too, and that there isn't anything we can't talk out."

He lowered his head and kissed her with all the passion and promise she'd longed for. Languor gave way to desire and the knowledge that he was hers. Now and always.

*   *   *   *   *

COMING NEXT MONTH

Take 4 bestselling love stories FREE

Plus get a FREE surprise gift!

Five unforgettable couples
said "I Do"...with a little help
from their friends—especially
me, Katie, always a bridesmaid.
But now, I'm...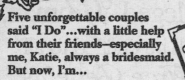

FINALLY A BRIDE
by Sherryl Woods
the fifth and final book of the Always a
Bridesmaid! series—only from
Silhouette Special Edition.

Katie's finally trading all those taffeta bridesmaid
dresses for a wedding gown of her own.
Gorgeous single dad Luke Cassidy proposed
marriage—a marriage of *convenience*....

Don't miss the big wedding!

Become a Privileged Woman,
You'll be entitled to all these Free Benefits. And Free Gifts, too.

To thank you for buying our books, we've designed an exclusive FREE program called *PAGES & PRIVILEGES™*. You can enroll with just one Proof of Purchase, and get the kind of luxuries that, until now, you could only read about.

BIG HOTEL DISCOUNTS

A privileged woman stays in the finest hotels. And so can you—at up to 60% off! Imagine standing in a hotel check-in line and watching as the guest in front of you pays $150 for the same room that's only costing you $60. Your *Pages & Privileges* discounts are good at Sheraton, Marriott, Best Western, Hyatt and thousands of other fine hotels all over the U.S., Canada and Europe.

FREE DISCOUNT TRAVEL SERVICE

A privileged woman is always jetting to romantic places.

When you fly, just make one phone call for the lowest published airfare at time of booking— or double the difference back!

PLUS—you'll get a $25 voucher to use the first time you book a flight AND 5% cash back on every ticket you buy thereafter through the travel service!